SPECIAL MESSAGE T

THE
(regis
was esta
research,
Exan
th

ABERDEEN
CITY LIBRARIES
www.aberdeencity.gov.uk/libraries

res   .

•   e

•   t

•   d

•   ,

•   n

•   l

You can h
by ma
Every co
would li

require further information, please contact:

THE ULVERSCROFT FOUNDATION
The Green, Bradgate Road, Anstey
Leicester LE7 7FU, England
Tel: (0116) 236 4325 WITHDRAWN

website: www.foundationulverscroft.com

Born in New York City, Amanda Eyre Ward studied fiction writing at the University of Montana. She spent a year visiting shelters in Texas and California, meeting immigrant children and hearing their stories, which proved to be the inspiration for writing *The Same Sky*. Now a critically acclaimed author, Amanda lives in Austin, Texas, where she currently writes every morning, and spends the afternoons with her children.

Visit her website at:
http://www.amandaward.com/

Twitter — @AmandaEyreWard

THE SAME SKY

In Texas, Alice and Jake own a barbecue restaurant. Hardworking and popular in their community, they have a loving marriage and thriving business — but Alice still feels that something is missing, lying just beyond reach. In Honduras, Carla is a strong-willed girl who's had to grow up fast, caring for her six-year-old brother Junior. After their grandmother dies, and violence in the city escalates, the two of them join the thousands of children making their way across Mexico to America, facing great peril for the chance of a better life. And eventually, the paths of Alice and Carla will cross . . .

Books by Amanda Eyre Ward
Published by Ulverscroft:

HOW TO BE LOST
FORGIVE ME
CLOSE YOUR EYES

AMANDA EYRE WARD

THE SAME SKY

Complete and Unabridged

ULVERSCROFT
Leicester

First published in Great Britain in 2015 by
Little, Brown Book Group
London

First Large Print Edition
published 2016
by arrangement with
Little, Brown Book Group
London

A catalogue record for this book is available
from the British Library.

ISBN 978–1–4448–2691–3

Published by
F. A. Thorpe (Publishing)
Anstey, Leicestershire

Set by Words & Graphics Ltd.
Anstey, Leicestershire
Printed and bound in Great Britain by
T. J. International Ltd., Padstow, Cornwall

This book is printed on acid-free paper

1

Carla

My mother left when I was five years old. I have a photo of the two of us, standing in our yard. In the picture, my mother is nineteen and bone-thin. The glass shards on the top of our fence glitter in the afternoon sun and our smiles are the same: lopsided, without fear. Her teeth are white as American sugar. I lean into my mother. My arms reach around her waist. I am wearing a cotton dress, a dress I wore every day until it split along the back seam. When the dress fell apart, my grandmother, Ana, stitched it back together with a needle and thread. Finally, my stomach pushed against the fabric uncomfortably and the garment was just too short. By that time, my mother was in Texas, and for my sixth birthday she sent three new dresses from a store called Old Navy.

When I opened that box, it seemed worth it — growing up without being able to touch my mother, to press my face against her legs as she fried tortillas on the gas stove. One dress was blue-and-white striped; on one, a cartoon girl ice-skated wearing earmuffs; the last was red. My friends with mothers — Humberto, Maria, Stefani — they stared at my outfits when I wore them to school. Maria could not take her eyes off the picture of the girl on my dress. 'She's ice-skating,' I said.

'Your mother?' said Humberto, scratching at his knee. Though Humberto was always covered in mud and didn't wipe his nose, I loved him and assumed we would be married in due time.

'Probably, yes, her too,' I said, lifting my chin. 'But I meant the girl on my dress. See? She wears earmuffs and gloves. Because it's cold. And the ice skates, obviously.'

'Ice is frozen water, but a lake of it,' added Stefani, whose mother had been my mother's best friend. Only my mother had been brave enough to leave, once my grandmother had saved enough for the *coyote*.

My mother sent money regularly and called every Wednesday at 12:45 p.m. Wednesday was her day off from working in the kitchen of a restaurant called Texas Chicken. I imagined her wearing a uniform the color of bananas. There was a movie we had watched standing outside the PriceSmart electronics store where an actress with red hair wore a banana-colored uniform and a tidy waitress hat, so when my mother described her work, I dressed her in this outfit in my mind. My mother told me her feet hurt at the end of her shift. My feet hurt, as well, when I wore the high-heeled shoes she'd sent. I needed shoes for running, I told her, and not three weeks later, a package with bright sneakers arrived.

There just wasn't much for any of us in Tegucigalpa. We lived on the outskirts of the city, about a twenty-minute walk from the dump, where the older boys and men from our village worked, gathering trash that had value. Humberto's older brother, Milton, left early in the morning. In the dark, he returned, his shoulders low with exhaustion and his hair and skin holding a rancid scent. Still — and to me, inexplicably — he had girlfriends. Though I had imagined what it would be like to kiss almost every boy in our village, I never closed my eyes and pictured Milton's lips approaching — it seemed impossible to want to be close to someone who smelled so bad. He was handsome, however, and supported his family, so there was that.

My grandmother took in laundry, and we always had enough food, or most of the time. Mainly beans. I had twin brothers who were babies when our mother left and were starting to walk around uneasily when I

3

turned six. They had a different father than I did, and none of our fathers remained in our village. Who knew if they were alive or dead and anyway, who cared.

This was how it was: most days our teacher came to school and some days he did not. When he had not come for three days, Humberto and I decided to go and find him at his house. We did not have bus fare and so we walked. We passed the city dump and watched the birds and the men and the boys. We split an orange Humberto had stolen from the market. We plodded through the hot afternoon, and around dinnertime (if you had any dinner) we reached our teacher's address.

The front door was open. Our teacher and his wife were dead, lying next to each other on the kitchen floor. The robbers had taken everything in the house. Our teacher, like me, had a mother in America, in Dallas, Texas, a gleaming city we had seen on the television in the window of the PriceSmart electronics store. The point is that our teacher had many things — a watch, alarm clock, boom box, lantern. Luckily, our teacher did not have any children (as far as we knew). That would have been very sad.

Humberto cried out when he saw the bodies. I did not make a sound. My eyes went to my teacher's wrist, but his watch was gone.

His wife no longer wore her ring or the bracelet our teacher had given her on their one-year anniversary. The robbers had taken our teacher's shoes, shirt, and pants. It was strange to see our teacher like that. I had never seen his bare legs before. They were hairy.

Humberto and I walked home. We were not allowed to be out after dark, so we walked quickly. We wondered whether we would get another teacher. Humberto thought we would, but said he might stop going to school and start going with his brother to the dump. They needed more money. They had not had dinner in two nights, and he was hungry.

'If you smell like your brother,' I said, 'I cannot be your girlfriend anymore.'

'Are you my girlfriend?' said Humberto.

'Not yet,' I said. 'Not ever, if you smell like Milton.'

'When?' asked Humberto.

'When I'm eleven,' I told him.

He walked ahead of me, kicking the dirt. He shook his head. 'I'm too hungry,' he said finally. 'And that's too long.'

'Race you,' I said. As we passed the dump, the birds shrieked: awful, empty cries. Yet the air on my skin was velvet, the sky magnificent with stars.

'Go,' said Humberto. We ran.

2

Alice

Jake and I weren't sure what to do about the party. Benji had sent out an e-vite to all our friends and the whole Conroe's BBQ staff before Naomi changed her mind about giving us her baby, and what else were we going to do with the afternoon? Just not show up? Just stay home and stare at Mitchell's empty crib? (An aside: it was also possible that Mitchell was no longer named Mitchell. Naomi might have changed her mind about that as well.) In short, we went to Matt's El Rancho on South Lamar.

Benji had gone all out. It was fantastic: a cake with blue frosting, baby presents piled high. There were margaritas and nachos, beef *flautas* and *queso flameado*. Jake ordered tequila shots like the old days. For about twenty minutes there was small talk, and then Lucy DeWitt said, 'Well? Where *is* the little cutie?'

'Oh, Christ,' I said. 'Well, it didn't work out, in the end.'

Jake raised his arm to signal the busboy,

pointing at our empty shot glasses. '*Dos más,*' said Jake.

'Oh, honey,' I said, putting my hand on Jake's shoulder and looking at the busboy apologetically. It was offensive to assume he didn't speak English, and also offensive to speak Spanish as badly as Jake did. I didn't speak Spanish at all, but I was going to immerse myself some summer soon.

'More tequila?' said the busboy.

'Yes, please,' I said.

Jake said, '*Sí, sí.*'

'What didn't work out?' said Benji, his brow furrowed. 'What do you mean, Alice?'

'The birth mother has forty-eight hours to change her mind,' explained Jake. 'And our . . . and we . . . ' Jake's eyes grew teary, and he put his palm over his face. I stared dully at the burn scar on his thumb.

'She took the baby back,' I said. 'She just . . . we had him at our house. We had him on the couch, and even on top of our bed. We put him in clean diapers and a swaddling blanket. He slept in his crib. And then she . . . she changed her mind.'

'They came and got him this morning,' said Jake.

'Oh my God,' said Lucy.

'Maybe she'll . . . maybe it's not . . . ' sputtered Carole, an English teacher at

7

Chávez Memorial High School, which was located three blocks from Conroe's BBQ.

'Anyone want a *flauta?*' I said, passing the tray. We didn't mention Mitchell again, and Jake and I left the restaurant without the baby gifts. We were pretty drunk, so Jake called Austin Taxi from the Matt's El Rancho parking lot. On the ride home, I rested my head on my husband's shoulder, watching the bright signs outside the cab window as we crossed the interstate to the Eastside: We Buy Gold Emporium, Churros Aqui!, Top Dawg's Bar and Grill. I told the driver to hang a right after Frank's Coin Laundry, where I brought our clothes every Monday when Conroe's was closed. Two blocks later, Jake said, 'Here we are.'

2215 Mildred Street — our home. We'd bought it from an elderly black woman who was moving to Pflugerville, joining the exodus of black families from downtown Austin's Eastside to the sprawling suburbs. It was a cottage, really: one thousand square feet of termite-nibbled hardwood. Jake and his father had painted the house a glossy white, added black shutters to the windows, erected a picket fence around the yard. I'd bought two brass lanterns to hang on either side of our hunter-green door. On one of our evening walks around the neighborhood, we'd found a broken porch swing. Jake used his welding equipment and a few cans of Rust-Oleum to restore the swing, hanging it on the front porch. In the backyard, we'd planted a lemon tree and a row of bamboo. We could be poster children for Eastside gentrification, but we were not ashamed. We'd made a home for ourselves on Mildred Street, same as the crazy lady at 2213 and the young family at 2217. Same as Omar Martinez, who lived across the street and worked at Juan in a Million, home of the best hangover breakfast in town.

★ ★ ★

Our house was dark. As the cab pulled away, Jake sank into the porch swing and I let myself inside. This had been, we'd vowed, the last chance. I was infertile, and our hopes for adoption had about run out. We had borrowed every last dime available to try to impregnate a kind but stoic surrogate in Detroit named Janeen. After Jake and I had flown to Michigan seven times, Janeen said — kindly and with stoicism — that she needed to close this chapter and move on. She was now pregnant with a Brooklyn man's sperm. I knew because I read her blog.

In the decade we'd been trying to have a

baby, our life had become a symphony of failure, almost rapturous with dramatic and dashed hopes. Pregnant women contacted us through our adoption agency, but then chose another couple, kept the baby, or (in one case) turned out to be a nut job who'd never been pregnant in the first place. I'd maintained a website advertising our cheery life and happy home (writing corny stories about how we'd met; what our days at Conroe's BBQ were like; and what sports, religion, and hobbies we'd teach our youngster), but though we received emails aplenty, none of the desperate people perusing the site had decided to bless us with a baby.

In the Detroit airport, after Janeen's announcement, Jake told me he was done. In the Fuddruckers restaurant next to Gate C17, he grabbed my hand and begged me to stop. Exhausted and low, I agreed to deactivate our adoption file, to close this chapter, to move on with grace, gratitude, and all that crap. We embraced, ignoring the stares of the other Fuddruckers patrons. I felt, when we were aloft and sailing through the sky toward Austin, that maybe we would be okay. But then Naomi had chosen us, and baby Mitchell had come.

The night before, I'd fed him. Small and dark, with a cap of black curls, Mitchell had opened his brown eyes and looked at me. 'I'm your mommy,' I said, tasting the precious words. I fit a bottle between his lips and watched him suckle, felt his body ease. As I held him, he passed with a tiny shudder from wakefulness to sleep. The moon outside his window was full. I was full. And then the agency called.

★   ★   ★

I went to Jake, brought him a beer. He opened it and drank, then I grabbed the can and took my own mouthful. The beer made the pain a bit less sharp, just for the evening. 'Oh, God,' I said, sitting down next to Jake, breathing the sultry air. The moon was still round and bright.

'I wish I knew what the point of this was,' said Jake. 'Or would you say *were?*'

'I don't know,' I said, 'and I don't care.'

'Fair enough,' said Jake.

People always seem surprised when they first meet me and Jake. He's good-looking and sure of himself, a blond former football star. In contrast, I'm nervous and dark-haired, more comfortable in the backcountry than at a country club. If Jake is a lion, regal and handsome, I'm a wren: fragile, easily spooked, ready to take flight. Somehow, though, it works. At night, I tuck myself into a ball, and Jake surrounds me, and I am warm.

In the moonlight, I saw a figure emerge from Beau and Camilla's house next door. 'Hello?' called Camilla. As she approached, I could see she was carrying a metal pot.

'We're drinking on the swing,' admitted Jake.

'I am so sorry,' said Camilla. Her Nigerian accent made the words especially sad somehow.

'Did you see them take the baby?' I asked.

Camilla hesitated, then nodded. Camilla and Beau had two daughters who had inherited their father's light hair and their mother's feisty attitude. 'I made soup,' said Camilla, unlatching our gate.

'Thanks,' I said. I made a move to stand, but Camilla shook her head.

'I'll put it in the kitchen,' she said, climbing our three front steps, opening the door. I heard her set the pot on our stove, and then she reappeared. 'We're here, if you need anything,' she said. 'I mean, we're there,' she said, pointing.

'Thanks,' Jake and I said in unison. We watched Camilla walk across the alley back to her home, where her family waited for her.

3

Carla

I was seven years old when a black car pulled up outside my grandmother's house (which was also my house, as I have mentioned). I had just returned from doing the washing in the river, rubbing my hands raw getting all the dirt out of strangers' pants or worse: the pants of people I knew! I hated the way my skin grew red and chapped, how I couldn't stop myself from pulling ribbons of dead skin from my fingers. But my grandmother was old, her own hands curled with arthritis that only a few sips of *guaro* would ease. She hung the clothes on a rusted wire, and my twin brothers toddled around her in circles, their feet caked in mud and God knew what else.

The car slid to a halt. I squinted against the sun, watched as a fat woman stepped from the driver's side and put her hands on her hips. Smoothing the front of her dress, my grandmother moved toward the woman. They spoke in hushed tones, my grandmother looking down and nodding, her lips pinched together in a way that meant she was scared.

My grandmother was not scared of much. She kept a crowbar underneath our pallet and had twice prevented robberies with her loud voice alone. No one who knew us would dare to steal from Ana — everyone understood that she was doing her best to raise her grandchildren in an uncertain world. But as jobs dried up and bad men grew more powerful than good, desperate strangers began walking farther from the city, toward neighborhoods like mine. They were looking for money or food, hoping for safety, searching for a way to remain in a place that had become unrecognizable.

My grandmother beckoned my brothers. Carlos and Paola (whom we called Junior) moved toward her with halting steps, pushing their chests forward and then throwing their feet out to catch themselves. Junior wobbled, flapped his arms like a chicken who had been disturbed, then fell on his naked bottom. He began to cry. Carlos waited, and when his brother dried his eyes, Carlos took his hand and helped him rise. They approached my grandmother and the fat woman.

'Only one,' said the fat woman. 'I would prefer the quiet one, but the choice is yours.'

'What's going on?' I said, standing up.

'Nothing to do with you,' said my grandmother. To the fat woman, she said,

14

'They cannot be separated.'

The woman shrugged. She wore a tight tank top and had large breasts. Her jean shorts said 'Sweetie' on the back pocket. I liked her shoes, which were called jelly sandals and could be bought at the market in the city.

'The mother only paid for one,' said the woman. 'I'm busy. Let's get this part over with before the whole neighborhood gets involved.' (It was true that people had begun to swarm around, sniffing trouble like a dog smells food.)

My grandmother looked very old. Her shoulders were bony underneath her faded dress, but her stomach pooched out. Her face was full of lines, especially around her mouth and across her forehead.

'Fine,' said the fat woman. 'This one. In we go.' She picked up Carlos, who did not make a sound. With her other arm, she unlocked the trunk of her car. 'Anything you want to send along?' said the woman. 'Diapers, water . . . ?'

'What are you doing with Carlos?' I said. I think a part of me already knew, and I felt a mixture of terror and envy.

'He's going to be with his mama,' said the woman. Carlos looked straight at me, opened his mouth. I shook my head, willing him to keep silent.

'Carlos!' cried Junior. 'Carlos!'

15

Carlos began to sob soundlessly, his face contorting into a mask of fear. He tried to climb out of the trunk, but the woman held him in place, her hand splayed on his head.

'Don't take him,' I said. 'Please. Take me instead.'

The woman looked me over appraisingly, taking in my dirty feet and callused hands. 'Nobody paid for you,' she said. And then she pushed Carlos down and slammed shut the trunk.

'He'll suffocate,' I told my grandmother, my voice brassy with panic. From inside the trunk, Carlos began to make terrible sounds.

'Carlos!' said Junior.

'He'll be fine,' said the fat woman. The sky above us was sand-colored, as flat and pale as desert. A lone grackle cawed, but there was no answer. I wished I knew how to stop time, to keep the shining car from departing with my brother inside. I put my hand to my mouth, bit hard on my knuckle. I wanted to do something, to feel something, to be the one leaving, and not the one left behind.

The fat woman got into her car and drove away.

'Hush, Junior,' said my grandmother. Junior had abandoned himself to sorrow: he was blubbering loudly, his face covered in tears and snot. Ana picked him up and he curled into her body.

'What about me?' I said.

'Keep hanging up the washing,' said my grandmother. But she came to my side and included me in her hug. 'God will watch over him,' said my grandmother. 'God will watch over us all.'

4

Alice

When I handed Principal Markson her Sweet Stacy sandwich (chopped beef, sausage, and coleslaw on a soft bun), she peered over her glasses for an extra moment. 'Alice,' she said, pushing the burgundy frames back into place, 'what in heaven's name are you doing here? Is the baby in the back somewhere? Asleep in a nest by the smoker?'

'The adoption didn't work out,' I said, the simplicity of my words belying my mangled heart.

'Oh,' said Principal Markson. 'Oh, Alice. I'm so sorry.' She held her paper bag in one hand and her phone in the other. The phone buzzed, but she did not look away from my face.

'Well, you know . . . ' I said, but could not think of a way to finish the sentence.

'I'm so sorry,' repeated Principal Markson.

'If you want, I can give you back the sweater,' I said, my voice wavering as I pictured the small garment, which Principal Markson had knitted herself. When she had

18

time to knit, I had no idea. Principal Markson, a heavyset black woman, was in charge of Chávez Memorial, which had been called Johnson High until the city shut it down the year before and replaced all the faculty. Most of the new teachers and many of the students came into Conroe's at lunchtime, though ever since the *Texas Monthly* 'Best BBQ' issue, we had to let them skip the line or they'd never get a morsel.

★ ★ ★

The *Texas Monthly* article had changed the length of the line outside Conroe's, but the rhythms of our days remained the same. Jake woke at 1:30 a.m. Despite the hoodlums who roamed our neighborhood at night — I was roused by the sound of gunshots (or maybe fireworks?) more than once — Jake insisted on walking to Conroe's, leaving me asleep. He passed two piñata shops (Raquel's Partyland and Ruth's Partyland), two bars (Club Caliente and El Leon), and four churches of various denominations. He'd promised not to walk through Metz Park or any alleys until daylight.

I'd bought Jake an antique Pasquini espresso maker during our honeymoon in Venice thirteen years ago, and the first thing he did every morning when he arrived at the restaurant (after telling Brendan, who tends the meat all night, to go home) was grind beans for a strong cup. Then Jake got to work trimming ribs, putting them in one of our five smokers by 3:30 a.m. The brisket cooks at a low temperature all night, hence the need for Brendan. Jake started the fires for the turkeys next, using post-oak wood and butcher paper covered in tallow harvested from the brisket he'd cooked the day before.

During the next few hours, Jake would sit out back in his favorite green lawn chair, keeping an eye on the smokers, perusing the three papers he had delivered to Conroe's every morning. We loved the *Austin American-Statesman* 'Life' section and the *New York Times* crossword puzzle; whatever squares Jake couldn't fill in, I usually could. This was the time-consuming art of barbecue: Jake monitored the wood fires, maintaining their temperatures, reading the smoke the way his grandfather had taught his father, who'd taught Jake.

People arrived around 7:00 a.m. to set up chairs and drink coffee in front of our small restaurant, sometimes waiting four or five hours for lunch. A man across the street started renting chairs (five bucks for the morning), and it was rumored that savvy

Austinites hired homeless men or students to stand in line for them, paying with money or meat. I never saw any evidence of this, though if I did I'd put a stop to it. That sort of behavior just isn't neighborly, and part of what we were striving for was a sense of community. There'd been two marriage proposals in line already, so I knew we were doing something right.

At nine, Benji and some of the other staff arrived to start slicing pickles and making coleslaw and potato salad. Before we opened, we made sure we had enough of all the sauces and that the bottles on the tables were topped off. We had a fridge full of pie delivered. (Bourbon banana pudding was the best, followed by Texas pecan.) Each table needed a roll of paper towels, crackers, and salt and pepper shakers.

Around ten-thirty I rolled in. I ate toast or yogurt at home; if I didn't eat before we opened, I wouldn't have a chance to take a bite until we closed. It was just nuts. I had a closetful of vintage dresses, and I usually wore one with a pair of boots. I put my black hair in a high ponytail, jamming a pencil in. On my fortieth birthday I'd gotten a makeover at Bobbi Brown, and though I had once worn nothing but Vaseline Intensive Care lotion and Chapstick, I now applied a light foundation, blush, crimson lipstick, and waterproof mascara. I shopped once or twice a month on South 1st, grabbing colorful old cowboy boots at Time & Again and dresses at Vintage Annie's or the Goodwill. I kind of had a look going, and I felt good about it. Jake wouldn't have noticed if I'd worn a sack.

The briskets, which cooked for eighteen hours at 250 degrees, came off around eleven, and Jake wrapped them in butcher paper and let them rest in the kitchen. I checked the tables and kitchen, then hung the 'Come On In' sign at 11:30. Either Benji or I propped the door open, beckoned to the early birds, and began making our way along the line with a pad of paper to take note of what everyone wanted. I made sure people understood how long they were going to have to wait, or if we wouldn't have any ribs or sausage by the time they hit the front counter. It had been Benji's idea to sell beer and Big Red to the people in line; every day he filled a plastic tub with ice and drinks and walked along the side of the restaurant, way into the parking lot and beyond. Folks made it a party, and it was pretty wonderful. I was proud.

We'd come a long way since meeting in New York City, Jake and I. I was going through chemo and studying English lit at Columbia and Jake was selling homemade beef jerky out of the back of his truck, putting himself through business school at NYU. Falling in love had been the first miracle, then my remaining alive, then the *Texas Monthly* article. We had so much, I reminded myself. So, so much.

★   ★   ★

'That's true,' said Principal Markson. 'You do, of course you do, but still.' I hadn't realized I'd been speaking audibly. Principal Markson had tears in her eyes. She had told me once that if she could make one of her teen mothers hand me her baby, she would.

But she couldn't.

She seemed rooted to her spot at the register, though a long line snaked behind her. Some youngster in a very clean cowboy hat raised his eyebrows and cleared his throat. I ignored him. 'How are things with *you?*' I asked.

'The usual,' said Principal Markson wearily. 'By the way, could we reserve a table next Monday for the Teen Suicide Prevention Task Force meeting?'

'Monday? Sure,' I said, though we didn't take reservations and she knew it.

'The Gang Prevention Task Force meeting is Wednesday,' said Principal Markson.

'Wednesday. You got it,' I said. These poor teachers needed all the breaks they could get.

'Markson, get a move on!' cried Officer Grupo, another regular. Principal Markson sighed, put her hand on mine, and squeezed. 'Hang in there, sweetheart,' she said. I nodded. When she walked away, I rubbed my eyes with the sleeve of my dress. Then I smiled at the youngster and took his order.

When we had run out of meat, I flipped the sign to 'Come Back Tomorrow!' and sat down heavily. I touched the tabletop, which was warm. The week we'd moved from our food trailer to the brick-and-mortar building, Jake's father had arrived from Lockhart with gorgeous pine tables he'd constructed from boards he'd found in the basement of his own (famous) BBQ restaurant.

Jake had gone for a nap or a swim at Metz Park. The hoodlums cleared out during the day, and the public pool was filled with screaming children and bleary mothers. Jake liked to do a cannonball or two into the deep end after a long, smoky morning.

As the staff cleaned up, I went into the back, made myself an espresso, and opened up the New York Times. I read the 'Dining and Wine' section and the book and movie reviews, then started trying to fill in the spaces Jake had left blank in the crossword. I checked my phone to find two messages from my father in Ouray, Colorado; one from my little sister, Jane, who lived with her husband and three kids in the house we'd grown up in; and one from Beau and Camilla inviting us to dinner. I sent Camilla a text, telling her we were busy, but didn't call anyone back home.

I had escaped my tiny town in Colorado as soon as I graduated from Ouray High School. Class valedictorian (number one out of twelve seniors, thank you very much), I was offered a full scholarship to Columbia and stayed on for graduate work. But as I was finishing my master's thesis, 'Recognition of Despair in the Essays of David Foster Wallace,' I found a lump in my right breast. My mother had died of ovarian cancer when I was eight and I'm a person who takes charge, so when the lump was found to be cancerous and a full genetic workup showed I had a BRCA1 mutation, I chose to undergo chemo and have my breasts removed. (That was an aggressive course of action, and I had no regrets. My sister, Jane, wouldn't even get the test that would show if she had the BRCA mutation that killed our mother. Instead, Jane married a man who would take over the family grocery store, bore three children, and lived in complete denial. She drove me insane.)

In the midst of all this, I met Jake. I was

walking through SoHo on my way to meet my Advanced Kierkegaard study group when Jake said, 'Hey! You! How about some jerky?'

I stopped. Nobody talked to me that way, not since my diagnosis (not ever). I'd been 'the girl whose mother died' all my life. Now I was 'the girl with cancer.' When a heavy guy in boots and a UT baseball cap yelled, 'Hey! You!' I took notice.

'Sure,' I said.

Jake laid out the various jerkies: beef, quail, venison. Hawaiian flavor, honey habañero, lemongrass chili, spicy beer. He cured the meat in his apartment, he said. I told him my dad was a butcher, so the plain beef had better be good.

'It is,' he said. 'Go on, try it.'

I took a bite. Jake was right — the jerky had a spicy tang that melted to a savory richness as I chewed. I nodded. 'Pretty fucking good,' I said. (Was this flirting? I could feel blood rushing to my face.)

'*Pretty* fucking good?' said Jake. He shook his head. 'You're a tough cookie.'

'That's true,' I said.

'Try the lemongrass chili quail,' he said. 'If that doesn't knock your socks off, I don't know what.'

It was a warm spring afternoon, and a recent rainstorm had allowed the streets to release their steamy tar scent. My mastectomy and reconstruction scars had healed, and the chemo hadn't made me sick yet. I wore a short pink skirt with espadrilles. The quail jerky was awesome.

'You love the quail,' said Jake. 'Am I right?'

I nodded, trying (and failing) to keep from grinning.

'What about a cold beer?' said Jake. 'Let's be honest, you're going to buy me out, so I might as well call it a day.'

I thought of my study group. We were reading *Concluding Unscientific Postscript*, and the latest pages argued that in order to live passionately you had to come to terms with the fact that death was inevitable. I could see my classmate Diane in my mind's eye, the grim set of her mouth, her lank hair. Diane had written what she called a 'Kierkegaard joke' on her notebook: *I shall certainly attend your party, but I must make an exception for the contingency that a roof tile happens to blow down and kill me; for in that case, I cannot attend.*

'Have you been to Pete's Candy Store?' said Jake. I shook my head. 'It's not a candy store,' he explained, 'it's a bar. What do you think?' He was so good-looking, so cheerful . . . I couldn't say no. So I said yes.

By nightfall, we were lying in the bed of

Jake's truck (he'd unrolled camping mattresses and pulled pillows from the cab), eating jerky and sharing confessions. Above us, the city lights were a constellation. I even told Jake about my cancer, and he said, 'Oh, who cares about boobs?'

'I care,' I said, and added, 'To be honest, my new boobs look better than my old ones.' My father, God bless him, had supplemented what my insurance paid toward reconstruction. *A free boob job*, I'd joked to my sister. *Lucky me.*

'Give me another kiss,' said Jake. I did. He smelled like home, in a way — like smoke and meat. People seemed to move around us so quickly in the dazzling night. I could hear Jake's heart as I nestled close. Later, on his squeaky bed, I let him touch the scars that ran across my chest. I didn't know what had come over me.

'Do they hurt?' said Jake.

'Not anymore,' I said. 'And they mean I'm safe.'

'Yeah?' said Jake.

'Who knows?' I said.

Jake kissed me deeply, and I was surprised to feel tears leak from the corners of my eyes.

By the time the chemo put me into early menopause and I told Jake I could never have kids, we'd been basically living together for a few months. 'We're young,' he said. 'Let's be in love for a while before we worry about anything, okay?'

'Okay,' I said, giddy at his mention of love.

When they were finished filling my body with potent, corrosive drugs, I was left cancer-free but exhausted, like a castaway tossed to shore. I didn't want to be anywhere near New York, the city where I had been sick. Once, Central Park had seemed romantic to me, a green wonderland where I could spend a lazy day, but now it was the place I took a cab through on the way to Sloan Kettering. Cabs in general were a problem — ever since I'd thrown up in one, I couldn't hail a taxi without feeling bile in the back of my throat. When I told Jake I wanted to leave the city, he said, 'My dad's talking about retiring. What if I took over his BBQ place in Texas?'

'Texas?' I'd said. I'd never been to Texas.

'Lockhart is pretty small,' said Jake, rubbing his chin. I loved his close-cut beard, loved to touch it myself. 'What about Austin?' he said, eyes lighting up. 'You'd love it, Al. It's completely different from New York. People smile at you.'

'I don't like it when people smile at me,' I said.

'They talk to you as well,' said Jake. 'Like, a lot.'

'Ugh,' I said.

'It's so warm,' said Jake. 'And it's legal to sell food from a trailer. You could help me, if you wanted. We could sell BBQ right along Barton Springs Road. That's a swimming hole, Barton Springs. You can lie on your back in the water and feel like a king. But that water is cold.'

'What about Fiji?' I said. I'd never been there either, but it sounded like somewhere different, somewhere no one would know me and what had happened to me.

'Austin,' said Jake firmly. 'And my family can host the wedding. We'll cater it ourselves, from our BBQ truck.'

'I think you're getting ahead of yourself,' I told Jake, my bighearted (and big-bellied) love.

'Say yes,' said Jake. 'To all of it. Why not? We'll adopt seventeen Chinese babies and live happily ever after.'

Why not, indeed? I shrugged. I'd studied English because I loved to read, but I didn't really want to teach or get a PhD. The thought of starting something tangible with Jake sounded fucking wonderful.

After all, in a world of countless perils, whom better to stay near than a man who could tame fire?

5

Carla

One morning, my grandmother didn't get out of bed. She had been moving slowly for some time, taking frequent naps, but I figured that was just what happened to people as they got old. She still woke each day before the sun, shaking Junior and me awake to serve us tortillas, beans, and hot coffee. (Fried eggs were a thing of the past now that we'd eaten the chickens, and the coffee grew weaker and weaker.) So it was a shock to squint against the rising sun, roll over, and find my grandmother beside me. 'Mamita!' I said, shaking her bony shoulder.

'I'm sorry, my love,' she managed. 'I'm going to sleep a little late today.'

'Are you sick?' I said, good and panicked.

'I may be sick,' said my grandmother. 'I just may be.'

I sat up, kicking my brother. 'Get up, you lazy ass!' I said.

'What did I do?' said Junior, rubbing his eyes, barely awake but ready to cry. He was a sweet boy, but so sensitive. I worried about

31

what the world held in store for him. It was as if God had sent his brother Carlos to protect him like a suit of armor, but now Carlos was absent, and Junior was soft, exposed.

'You didn't do anything,' I said, my fear curdling to anger. 'You never do anything! Help our grandmother! Boil some water.'

'Okay, I will,' whined Junior. As he started the stove, I turned my eyes resolutely away from my grandmother's wince. I stared at my brother's American underwear, at the faded image of a dog named Scooby-Doo on his bottom.

It was a Wednesday, and when my mother called that afternoon, I told her about my grandmother, wrapping the telephone cord around my wrist, watching the street beggars outside the window. 'Dios mío,' said my mother. 'I should be there to help you, little one. I'm so sorry. And poor Mami . . .' There was a silence as she gathered herself. Her voice was stronger when she said, 'Okay. I'll send money right away.'

'Can you come home?' I asked hopelessly.

'You know I cannot. Listen, I'll send as much as possible. You have to take her to the hospital. If you must take a taxi, take a taxi. Damn it, Carla.'

'It's not my fault!' I said.

'I know, little one,' my mother said,

softening. 'I just . . . I was trying to save money. I'm worn out.'

I didn't say anything. I tried to push down my anger, the sense that I had been abandoned, a fledgling left to founder in a disintegrating nest.

'How is Junior?' asked my mother.

'He's fine,' I said, my words coming out frozen as I tried to hide the neediness burning in my stomach.

'Did you get the T-shirts in the mail?'

'Sure,' I said. I didn't go to pick up clothes at the post office anymore. It was too dangerous. A girl with a package was a girl waiting to be robbed. But I didn't tell my mother this. What was the use in scaring her? I had already tried, and she had not come home.

'And you are going to school?' said my mother.

'Sure,' I lied.

★   ★   ★

When the money came to the Western Union a day later, Humberto helped me lift my grandmother from the pallet into a taxi. As I stood, feeling helpless, he pulled me toward him. 'I'll stay with Junior,' said Humberto, his voice warm in my ear. Junior, drawing in the mud with a stick, looked up and beamed.

33

'Put on some pants!' I told my brother.

At the hospital, a doctor told me that my grandmother had an infection in her blood. 'She needs to stay here, where we can watch over her,' said the doctor. In the hospital hallway, he went on, naming medications she needed. I told the doctor that my mother was in America and would pay for everything. But when he let me into her room, my grandmother had climbed from her metal bed and was sitting in a chair, dressed and ready to go. 'Take me home,' she said.

I explained the doctor's orders. She shook her head angrily. 'They don't know the first thing,' she said. 'I'm fine.' I helped her down the hospital stairs and held her hand, a bouquet of bones. We rode the bus back to the village. I knew she was going to die.

When my mother called the following week, I told her what had happened. 'You must come back,' I said. 'You need to buy the medicine and make her take it!' I could hear my mother breathing on the line. 'She just stays in bed all day,' I added. 'I have to watch Junior and cook . . . it's too much, Mami.' I bit my lip, a sob hot in my throat. For a moment, I let myself imagine that she would return. Her arms, her fragrant skin. 'Please help me,' I whispered.

'Oh, Carla,' said my mother. 'If I return to

Tegu, I'll lose my job. I might never get back to Texas. What will happen to us then?'

I told her I was ten years old and I did not know.

'Please don't be obnoxious,' she said. She said she would send every cent she could, all her savings, and that it was my job to make my grandmother go back to the hospital. 'I know I can count on you,' she said. 'You're my big girl.' When I hung up the phone, I saw that the Call Shop owner was looking at me.

'Stop complaining, you,' he said, crossing his arms over his chest.

I pushed open the door, the air a hot hand over my face, and I began to sprint toward the bridge that would carry me across the river. Past the glue sniffers, past the men in suits, past the buildings that blocked the sky and the graffiti-covered cement walls, past the barbed-wire fences and the skinny dogs, past the women selling their bodies and the women selling tortillas. I ran past the dump and finally reached the small road that led to my house, which — let's be honest — was a shack. As I approached home at last, my lungs tight and my thigh muscles scorched, I saw Humberto in the yard. My brother Junior was kicking a soccer ball, his face alight.

'You got him a soccer ball?' I said.

Humberto smiled.

My grandmother died that night, before any more money arrived and before I could talk her into anything. Junior and I were sitting next to her on the pallet. Junior was brushing her hair (which she loved, making a cooing sound at the pleasure of the bristles on her scalp) and I was massaging her hands and singing. She had not said much since returning from the hospital, but we knew she loved us. We knew she was worried about us.

When she stopped breathing, Junior's whole body shook. 'She's dead!' he cried. 'She's dead!' The words came out of his mouth squashed, as if being stepped on.

'Calm down, Junior,' I said. 'I will take care of you now.'

'You're a kid,' he cried.

I didn't say anything. Junior was correct.

When the sun spilled over the hills, sweeping away the menacing shadows, I went to the Western Union. I waited on the long line, avoiding the suspicious stares of the guards with guns. The man behind the bulletproof glass looked worried as he counted out my money: three hundred U.S. dollars. (Not even a fraction of what was needed to pay for a *coyote* to take me to America!) This was the sum total of my mother's years of working in the chicken restaurant. She had squirreled away tens and twenties, and now here were her labors being handed to me in crisp *lempira* bills. The banker sealed the money in an envelope and pushed it underneath the glass. His fingertips brushed mine and he whispered, 'Be careful.'

I tucked the packet in the waistband of my pants and walked out of the city as fast as I was able. It felt as if every hoodlum was watching me, ready to shove me down. Thankfully, I made it home safely. I put most of the bills in the coffee can my grandmother had kept buried underneath our pallet, and then I took Junior to the market and told him to choose anything he wanted. We ate three *tortas* each. We filled our arms with mangoes, oranges, and cold glass bottles of Fanta.

For two Wednesdays, I did not go to the Call Shop. I had begged my mother to come, and she had sent money instead. I myself went to Maria Auxiliadora Church and helped organize a funeral that my mother did not attend, paying for my grandmother to be buried next to my grandfather and covering her grave with plastic flowers, the kind that never wilt and never die.

6

Alice

Principal Markson called on Thursday and asked if I could come into her office for a meeting. 'Alice, I have a proposal,' she said. I wasn't sure what this meant, and the last thing I wanted was a teaching job, but I agreed to stop by. When I'd served the last quarter pound of meat, I flipped the sign and left Benji in charge of cleanup.

Feeling satisfied after a hard day's work, I walked into the blinding sunlight and turned left on East 11th, toward Chávez Memorial High School.

As hip as it had become, the Eastside was still a rough neighborhood, though that hadn't hurt Conroe's any. But it was one thing to drive to a dodgy part of town for brisket and another to spend your childhood in these streets. As I walked the three blocks to Principal Markson's school, I noticed yards containing broken toys and cars on cement blocks. In an alley, a group of young men huddled together, glancing up at me with cold eyes. A block later, a small boy with a fat face waved from behind the iron bars that covered his front window. I waved back.

Chávez Memorial was a faded brick building that could have housed a prison or a hospital. The parking lot was filled with late-model cars, some with metal panels that didn't match. One Honda had a blue body and two tan doors; its bumper sticker read, 'Proud to Be a Johnson High School Sophomore!'

Through wire fencing, I could see a dusty track and a set of bleachers on which a motley crew of boys sat and smoked cigarettes. A clump of girls stood underneath an oak tree, gesticulating wildly. Teenagers — their deep emotions, their unpredictability, the possibility that they could be armed — made me uneasy.

A large rectangle had been freshly painted on the front of the building to announce, 'Chávez Memorial High School at the Johnson High School Campus.' In front of the school, a six-foot marble block was ringed by stone benches that looked as if they'd been stolen from a graveyard.

I walked to the front door (I had never been inside) and pulled. The door was locked, so I pressed a red buzzer. Nothing happened. A police cruiser drove toward me, and when the window slid down, I saw that the driver was Officer Grupo, his eyes hidden behind mirrored sunglasses.

'Hey,' I said, squinting. 'Principal Markson told me to come by. It's locked.'

Grupo nodded, opened his door, and climbed out without turning off the engine. He carried the cool of his air-conditioned car in the folds of his uniform, and I had to stop myself from leaning toward him. He punched a code into the keypad. 'Can't be too safe these days,' he said.

'Jesus,' I said unthinkingly. 'This seems a bit much.'

'A bit much?' said Grupo, his words clipped short, as if by wire cutters. I turned toward him but saw only my flushed face in his glasses. He was white, about my age, with hair so light I could see his scalp. Despite his brash personality, there was a sweetness in him. He'd once given a Valentine — an actual paper card with a teddy bear holding a heart-shaped balloon on it — to Samit, who worked at Conroe's. I'd asked her if she was dating Grupo, and she said he kept asking, but she kept saying no. When I asked why, she'd held up her hands and said, 'No chemistry. And even though he's tall, he's kinda . . . puny. You know?'

Strangely, I understood what she was talking about. He was muscled, but defensively so, as if he was waiting to be beaten up by bullies.

40

'Three Chávez kids have been shot this year,' said Grupo, putting his hands on his hips. 'One right here in this parking lot.'

'Oh my God,' I said. Somehow when I'd thought about the gunshots I heard at night, I had connected them to 'bad guys,' thugs — not schoolchildren. I felt a sour shame in my stomach, suddenly embarrassed by my protected life, the attention Jake and I paid to barbecue.

'You know about walking the line?' Grupo said.

'You're not referencing Johnny Cash, I assume?' I tried to joke.

'It's a gang initiation. A kid walks along the line of members, and each beats the shit out of the new guy. He can't fight back. If he lives, he's in.'

'And they don't all . . . ' I said, my mouth growing dry.

'Nope,' said Grupo. 'They do not. Anyways, have a good one,' he said, walking back to his cruiser.

I stood outside the high school for a moment, letting Grupo's words seep in. I had seen the Chávez kids in Conroe's, after all, ordering sandwiches and Cokes, shoving each other, laughing. I felt for them — their preening, their acne-covered, animated faces. Christ, it had been hard to be a teenager in rural Colorado. It seemed so unfair that Markson's students had to worry not just about puberty and loneliness but also about guns and gang initiations.

Unnerved, I yanked open the door and stepped inside Chávez Memorial. The air was tepid, and on either side of me, rows of metal lockers stretched along a dim hallway. The school year was almost over: a banner reading 'Have a Safe and Happy Summer!' hung over a suite of rooms marked 'Principal.' I entered and asked an administrator for Principal Markson. She came out in a green pantsuit, rubbing lotion on her hands, greeting me with a gay 'Hello there, Mrs. Conroe!' As we entered her office, we passed two sullen girls sitting on folding chairs. One looked about six months pregnant, and (as always) I felt a twinge of anger and loss. I wrenched my gaze from the girl's belly. 'I'll be with you ladies shortly,' said Principal Markson.

The girls watched us, expressionless. Framed by Markson's doorway, they were a portrait of young misery. And then the principal shut her door. 'What have they done?' I asked.

'Who knows?' she answered, sighing, settling in behind a wide desk anchored by a dusty Dell Inspiron computer. 'Drugs, bad attitude, backtalk . . . ' She ticked off possible infractions. 'Knives, guns, hooliganism . . . '

'Hooliganism,' I murmured. The word seemed a relic from an easier time.

'Anything is possible,' said Principal Markson flatly.

'Oh,' I said. It was true that I'd usually cross the street when I saw a group of Chávez kids, but I'd never examined why. Some of the kids, who wore hooded sweatshirts and called to each other with deafening shrieks, did seem capable of anything.

'Which brings me to why I've asked you in,' said Principal Markson.

'Yes?' I said. The office was small, with a view of the front parking lot. Markson, who was single (as far as I knew), had a wall of photographs behind her: hundreds of kids' school portraits, Christmas cards, shots of choral concerts and sporting events.

'First of all,' said Principal Markson, 'are you okay?'

'What?' I said.

'Losing the baby . . . that must have been quite a blow. I was surprised you two didn't take some time off.'

'Time off?' I repeated dumbly.

She folded her hands in her lap and watched me. But I didn't want to sink into the grief. Jake kept bringing it up, how *sad* he was, how *disappointed*, wanting to commiserate and mope, but I was stronger than that. I knew that the only way to handle sadness was to push the fuck on through. 'I'm pretty busy,' I said. 'Let's move on.'

Principal Markson looked surprised, but pursed her lips and nodded.

'Okay.' She took a breath. 'Okay. We're getting our budget cut next year. If, of course, they don't close us down, but that's another issue for another day.'

'I'm sorry,' I said. Did she want Jake and me to donate money to the school? If so, she was in for a letdown. Our failed insemination efforts had emptied our savings, and even though Conroe's was doing well, we had little to spare.

'One of the positions we'll be losing is the full-time school psychologist. Juliet Swann — do you know her?'

I shook my head.

'She might be a vegetarian, now that I think of it,' said Principal Markson. 'Or a vegan? Not sure. There's usually a big yogurt labeled with her name in the staff refrigerator . . .'

'Well, that would explain it,' I said. There was an awkward pause. 'I'm sorry,' I ventured. 'But what does any of this have to do with me?'

Principal Markson clasped her hands. She paused, then said, 'Look. There are some kids

44

here in real trouble. They don't have guidance at home, and now they're not going to have as much guidance here. I'm reaching out to members of the community I think could be good role models. I'm hoping to create a Big Brother/Big Sister type of network, a way for adults to help at-risk kids at Chávez. Maybe eat lunch with them once a week, assist them with homework . . . '

'Oh, Principal Markson,' I said, 'I don't think so.'

'One girl I had in mind is Evian. Her mother is . . . let's just say *inconsistent*. Her father's out of the picture, and last year . . . well, she shot and killed her little brother. By mistake.'

My hand flew to my mouth. 'Oh, no,' I said.

'It was ruled an accident,' said Principal Markson. 'Her mother wasn't home. Evian called 911 herself and waited with her brother. He bled to death. She was showing him the gun, she said. It belonged to Evian's mother.'

I said nothing. My stomach churned and I wanted to get up and leave the room.

'Evian transferred from Travis, to get a new start. But she often skips school,' said Principal Markson. 'There's no one to keep an eye on her, check in. She's depressed,

45

most likely, and who knows what else. She doesn't have anyone. No one. I know you're busy, Alice, I do. But I just thought I'd ask. If you could just have lunch with Evian once a month? Just come to the cafeteria and sit with her for twenty minutes. I wouldn't ask if I had . . . other resources.'

'Lunch is a busy time,' I said.

Principal Markson stood. 'I understand. I hope you don't mind my giving this a shot. I've got a list of kids like Evian, and I'm just trying to do what I can to help them.'

I nodded, standing. Principal Markson smiled as I departed, but I could see exhaustion etched into her features. 'Have a good one,' she said, echoing Officer Grupo's salutation.

'I'm really sorry,' I said.

'What can you do?' she replied. I walked away from her office feeling like a jerk. But what did I have to offer a depressed teenager? Nothing, I told myself. Still, as I left the school and walked toward Conroe's, waving at Grupo in his cruiser, I felt a certain stirring. I tamped it down, pushing the girl from my mind. At Conroe's, I climbed into my Ford Bronco (with newly upholstered leather seats — an anniversary gift from Jake) and drove toward Mildred Street. Jake would be waking up soon, and I felt like kissing him until my thoughts receded.

7

Carla

As I had hoped, on my eleventh birthday Humberto asked me to be his girlfriend. By this time we had both stopped going to school and spent our days at the dump. Not many girls could handle the smell and the aggression, but I am not like other girls. As I've mentioned, my mother was in America, which gave me strength.

In the years my mother had been absent, her voice had grown raspy, hoarse. She sounded old. During one Wednesday call, my brother Carlos (now in kindergarten at Campbell Elementary School in Austin, Texas) mentioned 'the baby.' I asked him, 'What baby?' but my mother made him get off the phone. I asked her, 'What baby?' and she said to please stop asking so many questions. Was she married? I asked her, and she said, '*Dios mío*, no.'

* * *

Each morning we walked to work in a group, our garbage bags over our shoulders:

47

Humberto, me, some other boys. People lived at the dump, so we tried to arrive as close to dawn as possible to fill our bags before the piles were all picked over and you had to touch the needles or dig through shit to reach anything with value. Toward evening, trucks arrived, paying us handfuls of *centavos* for our hauls.

Some of the girls I knew had started sniffing glue. Some had become prostitutes. This is not a euphemism. No one was hiring you to do their laundry, not anymore. There were few jobs for men and no jobs for women. The robbers had become increasingly violent. I could go into more detail, but the point is that times were very hard. A woman had something to sell, and many did.

I did not.

I guess it was my grandmother's Catholic doctrine, and the fact that my mother sent us enough money to survive. I believed that sex was something I would save for marriage. I lay in bed some nights, praying that I would remain a virgin. For some reason, I felt that this was out of my control.

On my eleventh birthday, I made fifty *centavos*. Walking home, Humberto and I lagged behind. Ever since I had started gathering trash myself, Humberto's odor did not affect me. He walked very close, and I thought about him putting his fingers beneath my chin, tipping my head up, and placing a soft kiss on my lips. (I had seen this slow buildup in American movies.)

At the door to my house, Humberto paused. His shirt was worn thin as silk, and his body was wiry, his skin scratched and dirty but to me, perfection. 'Carla,' he said.

'Yes?' I said. I could hear my brother shuffling behind the door. After my grandmother died, Junior stopped going to school. No matter how much I raised my voice, telling him that he needed to educate himself, that he was too young to be left alone, he did not listen.

'Carla?' My brother's voice sounded scared. But I ignored him: Humberto had a dreamy look on his face. *This is the moment,* I thought.

'I was hoping . . . ' said Humberto. Was he going to ask me to marry him? It was too soon for that. And he had so little money. I wanted to kiss Humberto, but I was not sure I wanted to stay here, in Tegu. Even with him.

'You could be my girlfriend, if you wanted,' said Humberto in the nonchalant voice he used when he was afraid but wanted to sound unafraid.

His face was as familiar to me as Junior's. He had dark eyes, and hair that curled along the sides of his face unless he caught it in a rubber band. 'I do,' I said. He sighed with relief, his smile showing his nice teeth.

'I won't have sex with you,' I said. 'I mean, I want to stay a virgin until my wedding.'

'I know,' said Humberto, who knew everything about me.

'I guess I've always loved you, you idiot,' I said.

'I know,' said Humberto. He cupped the back of my head with his large hand. 'Good night,' he said. He pressed the side of his face to mine, his skin soft and warm. But there was no kiss.

'Good night,' I said. I watched Humberto walk off, admiring his long stride, his thin but muscled back, and then I whispered to Junior to open the padlock and let me inside.

In the middle of the room was a new dress. It was aqua, and made from some amazing fabric that fell across my hands in waves.

'It came today,' said Junior. He sounded strange. 'Stefani brought it to the house.'

'Have you been crying?' I asked.

He shrugged. 'I'm hungry,' he said.

We had so little food by this point. I made a paste of flour and water, and as we ate, I looked at the dress. When would I wear such a thing? What did my mother think my life was like? You could not eat a dress.

Still, after I scratched Junior's back and he fell asleep, I slipped from the pallet and took off my clothes. I pulled the garment over my head. It fit me perfectly. Our mirror was cracked and rusty, but I could tell I looked like a supermodel.

'Happy birthday,' I said to the girl in the mirror.

8

Alice

As soon as I stepped off the plane in Montrose (an hour and a half from my Colorado hometown), I realized I should have left my vintage skirt and red leather cowboy boots at home. Funky wasn't really a thing in my family. My sister was waiting by the gate in high-waisted jeans, sneakers, and a functional anorak; her three boys wore athletic shorts and T-shirts.

Jake, who had recently grown a moustache, gripped my hand tightly. My father, in his John Deere hat and twenty-year-old parka, stood with his hands on his hips behind Jane and her kids. 'Your dad scares me,' whispered Jake.

I squeezed his hand back. Jane came running, her smile huge and warm. She looked the same as when she was six, with her wheat-colored hair cut shoulder length, bangs straight across her full face. She hugged me so tightly I struggled for breath, and then she was wrapped around Jake, who shot me a look of thrilled panic. 'Boys!' Jane yelled to her sons. 'Come give your aunt Alice and uncle Jake a hug!'

We were swarmed by skinny arms and I breathed in the smell of dirty sneakers. Tears came to my eyes, but I brushed them away. 'I'm so sorry,' said Jane. 'Oh, Alice, I'm so sorry.'

'Yeah,' said Jake sadly. 'It's been — '

'Where's Dennis?' I asked, to change the subject.

'What do you think?' said Jane. 'He's running the store.' My parents had taken over the town grocery store, Hill's Market, from my grandparents. My father, Joshua Hill, learned from his father how to be a butcher. He'd met my mother while hiking in the Bob Marshall Wilderness. Before they had us, my mom and dad hiked the Appalachian Trail and the Pacific Crest Trail. They backpacked in Mexico's Copper Canyon and ascended Machu Picchu. Then they returned to Ouray, took over the store, and never looked back. My mother told me that when Jane and I were born, all her dreams had come true. I still remember her voice breaking a bit as she said, 'Now I get to enjoy.'

After she died, my father became quiet, leaving us with his parents and taking off for days at a time to go into the backcountry. He hunted and fished, teaching us to do both as well. The first time I brought Jake to Ouray, I challenged him to climb Mount Sneffels, my favorite Colorado fourteener. He barely made it to the picnic lunch before begging me to halt.

'You've got to reach the peak, or try,' I admonished him, using my father's stern tone. 'You can't just stop!'

'Watch me,' Jake had said, settling in a grassy spot and pulling a salami sandwich from his backpack.

Now he conferred with my father about the July 4 brisket; the men planned to stay up all night July 3. Years before, Jake had built a smoker in Jane and Dennis's backyard, winning over all our nephews by letting them try out his welding equipment. In the airport, my father clapped his hand on Jake's back, leaning in and saying something about the dry rub. 'Hi, Dad,' I said, under my breath.

'You know how he is,' said Jane.

*   *   *

When Jake and I had booked our July trip to Colorado, we thought we'd be bringing Mitchell to meet the family. When those plans changed, Jake convinced me we needed a break from the Texas heat anyway and should keep our reservations. We'd already given everyone at Conroe's the week off, he insisted. I loved Colorado but found it full of uncomfortable memories and relationships that stressed me out. It was hard not to compare myself with Jane. I was jealous of her kids, and being around her made me question my decisions. At the same time, I worried about my baby sister. No matter how much I pushed, she refused to have the genetic screening that could save her life. I'd have a talk with Dennis this visit, I decided.

★ ★ ★

Jake and I were staying in the apartment above Hill's Market. It was where our family had lived when Jane and I were babies, before our parents bought the Oak Street house.

Now it was rented out or used for visitors. (Dennis had a large family in nearby Gunnison.) As Jake and I lay in bed for the first night of our three-night stay, I stared at the familiar striped wallpaper. 'It does smell good here,' I whispered. 'Cleaner, or something. It smells like snow, even in July.'

'Don't get any ideas,' warned Jake.

'Don't worry, my love,' I said. Still, as we spent our first morning making pancakes at Jane's house, getting used to the constant activity as the boys whirled through the kitchen like tumbleweeds, I felt a yearning. It wasn't that I wanted to live in Colorado, of course, though I adored the way the sun shone on the mountains, loved the way the water was always ice-cold coming from the faucet, felt safe and happy lying on the lawn with no thoughts of chiggers. Maybe it was Colorado. Who knew?

★   ★   ★

That evening, July 3, Jane and I left our husbands and father in the yard with growlers of beer and the slow-cooking brisket. Jane said I could sleep over, as Dennis would be up all night, but I declined. I walked from Oak Street to Main Street, past the old Randolph house, where my first boyfriend had lived, and the Western Hotel, where I'd had my first legal beer. I felt both nine years old and seventy. I was a visitor here now, and I always would be. I would never be a Colorado mother. I missed my own mother. I stood on the bridge above the rushing Uncompahgre River for a while, feeling melancholy.

The apartment above the store had a deck that overlooked Twin Peaks. I took a cup of hot tea outside and curled up in a chair. I remembered sitting on my mother's lap in this same place. Was she somewhere? Could she see me? 'Mom?' I said aloud. I blinked back tears, feeling stupid. Somehow I'd thought she'd send me a sign — a shooting star, an owl calling out — but of course there was nothing. She was gone.

9

Carla

I suppose I always knew I would ride The Beast to America. My mother told me not to come, but she didn't understand what life had become in Tegucigalpa. I found it hard to sleep for fear of robbers. A boy I'd known since childhood, Oscar, told me I had to pay him protection money or risk being raped and beaten. But it wasn't until what happened with Junior that I knew it was time to go.

Everyone was aware I had a mother who sent money. Junior and I were targets, because most people had nothing. Some robbers were getting organized, selling drugs, but when business was slow they became roving gangs, sending boys like Oscar to take from those who had any small thing.

Junior, as I've said, spent much of his time alone. On occasion he came with me to the dump, but he barely gathered enough to help at all. He took to sitting outside the house instead of inside. At six years old, he was skinny, with long legs and a sunken chest. He started to have opinions (throwing a bowl of paste on the floor, saying it was 'shit') and desires ('I want to be the Terminator and kick everyone's ass!'). He set his jaw in such a way that he looked like an angry adult. Sometimes he would surprise me on my walk home, just appearing by the side of the road in the dangerous purple twilight.

'I needed to get out,' he would mutter when I admonished him. It was painful to look at Junior — he was so hard and hungry — and to remember myself at six, beloved by my grandmother, clad in new American clothes.

One night Humberto and I walked home as always, weary and dirty but holding hands. I was still waiting for my first kiss. As we walked farther from the dump, the awful smell faded and it seemed possible to remember that we were young. I had turned twelve by this point, and I felt very tired. This is hard for an American to understand, but it felt like my life was over. In my village, some married at my age, and soon became mothers.

Humberto brought me joy. This was all the happiness I had: the way he looked at me and how this made me feel. If you pressed down one of the curls on his head, it sprang back up. This was what Humberto was like in general. You could not keep him flat. Oh, the feel of his fingers around mine. I knew — I thought I knew — we would marry in the Maria Auxiliadora Church, in a ceremony that was long enough to make Junior fidget in his pew, but also glorious. We would move into the same house — into the same room! — and I would greet my Humberto each evening with a kiss and a hot meal. In this way — sitting next to each other, the sunset burning from marmalade orange to violet to black, sipping milky coffee, holding hands — we would grow old.

But I wasn't ready to be old yet.

So much was mixing in my mind that night; it was confusing. There was the girl I had been, the child my brother Junior was not allowed to be. There was sadness for having to pick through garbage. There was hope for the thrilling kisses Humberto and I would share, and also the ways of our bodies coming together. I knew the basics, of course, but had been told by Stefani that my own body would do things I could not yet understand. (Stefani had been seduced by an older boy, a man, eighteen. He took her from her family and into the city. I had not heard from her in months.)

Humberto's brother, Milton, had tried to get to America the year before. He had told us that he would go to Arizona, where the crossing was easiest because there were fewer immigration officials. Obviously, none of us knew how to get to El Norte, not really. We had heard things. We had seen things. Some of us had relatives in America (like me). Some had money for *coyotes*. Some paid *coyotes* and were caught by *la migra* anyway. Some people did not want to leave, the old or secure, but many of us dreamed of escape, of money and food and a complete family.

But back to Humberto's brother, Milton. He set off at dawn with a dozen water jugs and three pairs of pants and three shirts on. All his money was in his underwear. I watched him go. He didn't say goodbye to me, and why would he? He was seventeen. He could spend his life in the dump or he could try to reach El Norte.

Milton was gone for two weeks before he was caught and brought back to Tegu in a small van. He'd never even made it past Guatemala. Police had raided a park where he was sleeping, gathering his strength for the journey through the Guatemalan jungle to Mexico.

Getting into Mexico, Milton told us, was the most important thing. Once you made it into Mexico, you could pretend you were Mexican and they would only deport you back to southern Mexico. All your trouble

61

would not be for nothing. But if you were caught in Honduras or Guatemala, you would start all over. Milton was discouraged, but a week in the dump convinced him to try again. This time he was gone for almost a month. He came back skinny and with many stories. People fell and were crushed by the Train of Death, he told us. Gangs lay waiting to kill you, to steal your clothes. Still, the gleam in his eye told the truth: he was gone again three days later, leaving his pregnant girlfriend in tears. Two weeks later, he was returned to us — dropped off in the city again.

This time he started with the glue. You can get a baby-food container with glue at any store, and breathing it takes away pain. The Resistol is cheap, but eventually people will rob their own grandmother to obtain it. I have never seen anyone stop using glue once they have begun. Never. Not once.

Humberto and I made a pact when we were young. We saw the yellow-mouthed zombies that replaced our friends, and one night Humberto cut a line down the center of his palm with a broken Fanta bottle and made me do the same. We pressed our bloody hands together and promised each other we would never sniff Resistol. I have kept my promise.

But back to Milton. He stayed in the village

until his girlfriend gave birth, and when the baby was a few months old, he left again. Milton was gone for months this time. We assumed he had made it. His girlfriend waited for news, money, maybe even clothes for their baby girl.

Instead, Humberto answered the door one morning and a social worker told him Milton was dead. His bones had been found in the desert outside Tijuana. He had almost made it to California. His remains were returned and we held a funeral. In the front pew, Milton's girlfriend held his daughter, Aylyn. Neither cried, but Humberto's eyes grew wet when he placed his hand on his brother's coffin.

★　★　★

One night, walking home from the dump, I told Humberto that I was worried about Junior. I did not know what he was up to all day, but I knew he no longer stayed at home, where he was safe. Humberto told me he would think carefully about how to help Junior. (He was already helping his elderly mother and his brother's girlfriend and daughter. To be clear: he was feeding four people by gathering garbage.)

I think Humberto felt it was selfish to go. It

was true that most of the ones who left were the braggarts, the most macho boys. My own mother had made it, but she had gone with a *coyote*. The thousands of U.S. dollars a *coyote* would cost (three thousand for a male *coyote*; six or more for a female, who would hopefully be less likely to rape you; ten thousand for a plane trip with papers) were not possible anymore. Not for us, anyway.

Still, we thought about it: America. We thought about it all the time. I'm sure you think you can imagine what we dreamed of — buffet tables of food, video game arcades. I will tell you my secret. When I dreamed of America, I imagined lying down in a large green field, watching my mother unpack a picnic dinner. The basket was filled with anything I could dream of, but before we ate my mother pulled me close to her. I could remember her smell: faintly floral, rich, bready. She ran her fingers through my hair, pressed my face to her chest. 'I love you,' she said. We were warm in a circle of sunlight. 'My daughter, I am here,' she said. That was it, the sum of my dream.

★　★　★

Humberto dropped me off at our dwelling, which my grandfather had built after

64

Hurricane Mitch consumed everything in Tegucigalpa. I had been a child when the river rose up and covered the city, leaving mud and misery in its wake. My grandfather was a shopkeeper, and he was able to salvage enough to pay for wooden slats and construct one room. He walked through the thigh-high mud to find a tin roof, which he weighted down with rocks. It's said that Tegu never recovered from Hurricane Mitch, but there we were, Junior and I. Like most of our neighbors, we did not have running water or a bathroom, but we did have a few bushes outside where we could relieve ourselves.

Why God made certain decisions, I could not even dream of knowing. God only gave my grandparents one child — my mother — though they had yearned for more. God sent Hurricane Mitch to Honduras, and yellow glue. Yet He also gave us the stars, the feel of the cool night on our faces. He gave me my brothers, and the way I felt when Humberto looked at me. I believed God watched over me. I was lucky in this. Many people I knew feared that God had forgotten them.

That night, the front door was closed, which was a relief. (I was always afraid it would be kicked in, our pallet and small collection of cookware gone.) But when I whispered for Junior to let me in, he did not answer. I shoved the door and it fell open. I scanned the room; all seemed in place. On the pallet, there was a lump of blankets. I approached, put my hand on my brother's back. He was breathing deeply, fast asleep. I closed the padlock and lay next to Junior, my arm around his small body. I knew then what the end of hope smelled like: yellow glue on your brother's breath.

10

Alice

There's the ice festival, of course, and New Year's Eve — when people drive their Jeeps into the Amphitheater, place flares on them, and drive down Route 550, a winding dragon of light into town — but in Ouray, Colorado, the Fourth of July is the biggest event of the year. I woke up alone in the lumpy bed that had been my parents', took a quick shower, and headed to my sister's house in my red-white-and-blue flared skirt and cropped blouse. (And my red boots.)

Jane was already pulling the second sheet of cinnamon buns out of the oven. (The first lay scavenged on the stove.) It didn't look as if she'd showered, and her pajamas were an unflattering maroon. 'Hello, hello!' she cried when I slid open the screen door to the kitchen and entered. 'Wow, look at you,' she said tartly. 'Lipstick and everything.'

'Thanks,' I said, though her words hadn't exactly been a compliment.

'Here,' she said, handing me a plate. 'Coffee? Eggs?'

'Hell, yes,' I said, savoring the hot cinnamon bun. 'God. This tastes exactly like Mom's.'

'It's her recipe,' said Jane, 'and her pan.'

'Wow,' I said brightly, awkwardly.

'Please, let me pour your coffee,' said Jane. 'Don't strain yourself.'

'I'm sorry,' I said.

'It's fine,' said Jane, through gritted teeth.

'What's going on?' I asked.

'I'm just tired,' she said. She ran her fingers through her hair. Her youngest, Benjamin, ran into the kitchen holding out an empty plate.

'Dad wants more!' he announced.

'I'll get it,' I said, standing up. 'Go take a shower, Jane. I can take over in here.'

'Ha!' said Jane, wresting the plate from my hands.

When Benjamin had run back outside, Jane sank to the kitchen floor.

'Jane!' I said, alarmed.

'Just let me sit,' she said. 'I've been standing since five.'

'Why didn't you ask me to help?' I said.

'I don't want to have to *ask*,' spat Jane.

I filled a mug with coffee and cream, the way she liked it. I handed Jane the mug and sat next to her. The linoleum floor was dusted with crumbs and muddy footprints. 'Three is too many kids,' said Jane dully.

'Give me one,' I said.

We both started to laugh. 'Which one?' said Jane.

'Any one,' I said, suddenly sad. 'I just want one.'

Jane pulled me close.

'Is everything okay with you guys?' I said.

'Not really,' said Jane.

'What is it?'

'Not today,' said Jane, standing up.

'Is it Dennis?' I asked. 'Is it Dad?'

'I *am* going to take a shower,' said Jane. She set her mug on the counter. 'And I don't use cream anymore,' she said. 'I'm trying to be on a goddamn diet.'

'Mom said 'goddamn'!' cried Gilmer, appearing in striped pajamas.

'Gilmer!' I said, trying to sound like a mother.

'Well, she did say 'goddamn,' Aunt Alice,' explained Gilmer earnestly. 'We're not allowed to use swear words in this house.'

'I think I see the Tickle Monster,' I said.

'No!' shrieked Gilmer, running outside.

'Oh, yes,' I said, starting the chase.

Fifteen minutes later, I collapsed in a deck chair by the barbecue pit. My father was snoring in the hammock, and Dennis and Jake looked grizzled, half drunk, and very happy. I put my hand on my husband's knee and he covered it with his own. 'How's that brisket?' I asked.

'Looking good,' said Jake. 'Looking very, very good.'

'That's true,' said Dennis, nodding.

'More Tickle Monster!' called Benjamin, running toward me. I held up my hands.

'No more,' I said, shaking my head.

'More, more, more!' yelled Gilmer, his voice going thin, as if he was about to start crying.

'Sorry, honey,' I said.

'You can't start them up and quit,' said Dennis evenly.

'Oh,' I said, chagrined. I was sweaty and annoyed, sick of running across the lawn in my tight-fitting boots. I wanted more coffee and some scrambled eggs. 'Can you do it?' I asked Jake.

'Nope,' said Jake, sliding down in his lawn chair and pulling his baseball cap over his eyes.

'Get up,' said Dennis in a nasty tone.

I got up.

'Yay! Tickle Monster!' said Benjamin.

'Try to catch me now!' said Gilmer, pulling his pajama pants down and peeing in the yard. The parade-goers were assembling a block away, and a firefighter in full gear

70

pointed to Gilmer and whooped.

'Somebody's naked!' cried fourteen-year-old Rick, turning on the garden hose.

It was 7:55 a.m.

11

Carla

In the middle of the night, Junior stirred. I had been dreaming of playing with him in the mud, tossing the Frisbee an aid worker had given us. In the dream, Junior's belly was round, his legs fat. My grandmother cooked red bean soup in the metal pot that had been stolen years ago. It was a shock to open my eyes and see my skeletal brother staring at me. 'What is it?' I said.

'I'm hungry.'

I sighed. There was nothing left of the money my mother had sent. I had eaten a rotten piece of chicken at the dump and had vomited for days, so I had been wary of bringing Junior scraps of food. In the kitchen we had only empty space, but I stood. 'Go back to sleep,' I said. 'I'll make you something very delicious.'

His gaze was blank.

'Are you sniffing Resistol?' I asked.

He shook his head, but would not meet my eyes.

'It will hurt your brain,' I pleaded. 'It will

kill you, Junior. You can never go back once you begin.'

'I know,' he said sadly.

I went to the cabinet. We had a bit of cooking oil left. I had eaten a stale tortilla that morning, trading a wire spool for the food. Now I berated myself for not saving a bit for my brother. He rose from the pallet and I gathered him in my arms. 'I will take care of you,' I said. He nodded, his face impassive. I wondered if he believed me.

I did not want to leave the house. I knew it was stupid — I knew the things that happened in the dark, and you can imagine them, too, I am sure — but I could not let my brother starve.

'Don't let go of me!' said my brother as I stepped away.

'Hush,' I said. 'Stay here.' I opened the door.

My home — silver hills rising to meet a dazzling sky. I felt heavy with the knowledge that the beauty was a mirage. Gangs, some made up of strangers, many consisting of boys I knew, roamed the streets. They had guns, these boys. They killed out of boredom. There were robbers, and there were people like me: so hungry that we would do what we knew was wrong to survive. There were men who wanted a woman's body and did not care what the woman felt. I could find a man like this, just sell a few minutes of myself for food. I tried to think of another option.

I walked in the black toward Humberto's house. If he had anything, he would give it to me. I stepped quietly, almost screaming when a mangy cat brushed against my leg, then ran away. I was shaking and my heart beat fast. This was no way to live. It came to me like a lightning bolt: *This is no way to live.* I walked more quickly. When I arrived at Humberto's, I peered in the window and saw that everyone was asleep.

I didn't know what to do. It wasn't fair to wake Humberto and his family. We were all hungry, for God's sake! I leaned against the cement wall, slid down into the dirt outside his house, hugging my knees to my chest. I wished for my mother, but I had no money for a phone call. My mother had said she would send money the week before, but the man at the Western Union insisted there was nothing in my name. I felt a creature — an ant? — crawl along my calf, then to the top of my kneecap.

There was no point in crying. I was a pragmatic girl. My brain scanned like a radio, looking for a plan. I could try to break into a house, to steal food. I could walk into the city and stand outside the Western Union until they opened. For a minute I thought about sniffing glue myself, just to quell my panic and fear. Instead, I stood up and knocked on Humberto's door.

'Who is it?' asked dead Milton's girlfriend, Gabriela.

'It's Carla,' I said.

Humberto opened the door. 'What's going on?' he said. He rubbed his eyes.

'What's going on is that I'm going to America,' I said. 'Are you in or are you out?'

Humberto shook his head. 'You're crazy,' he said.

'Can I please have a small bit of food?' I said. 'Junior is so hungry. Just this last time.'

'Don't give it to her,' yelled Gabriela, the witch. Though she had been kind to me when I became a woman, even giving me a menstrual cloth to use (and wash each night), I knew Gabriela envied my youth and the way Humberto loved me. She guarded each scrap he brought home from the dump. If I were the jealous type, I would be jealous. But I knew what was meant to be.

Humberto rummaged in the cupboard, pulled out a heel of bread.

'Thank you,' I said.

'You idiot,' said Humberto. 'Are you really leaving?'

'In one week,' I told him, making the

decision so easily it must have been the right one. 'This is not a life,' I said. 'You can come with me, or I will leave you behind.'

'You idiot,' repeated Humberto, shaking his head. And then he gripped my face with both his warm hands, and he kissed me.

12

Alice

The Fourth of July parade — historic cars, the fire truck, baton twirlers, and a 4-H float — lumbered down Main Street, leaving confetti, candy wrappers, and sunburned spectators in its wake. Jane's kids ran home by themselves, their pockets full of Jolly Rancher candies and plastic beads, while we folded the camp chairs and hauled them up Oak Street. The altitude (or maybe the festivity) was making me tired. 'Remember when we used to have a float?' I said.

My dad laughed. 'Your mom loved that sort of stuff,' he said.

'What? Parades?' I asked.

'She loved using a glue gun,' said my father.

'Who doesn't?' said Jane.

'She loved pasting crepe paper onto poster boards,' said my father. Jane and I exchanged glances: it was rare for our dad to talk about our mom.

'She did?' I prompted.

'She loved modeling clay,' he said. He nodded soberly, then said, 'Well, see you later.

Told Bill I'd stop in for coffee.' He turned on his heel and strode away from us, toward the Episcopal church, raising his arm in farewell.

'Who's Bill?' I said.

'The new pastor. He's young,' said Jane. 'How come I don't remember Mom using modeling clay?'

'She'd make us snakes, little snakes out of clay,' I said. 'And she'd make those signs for the store. Remember? 'Fresh Strawberries' or 'Ortega Taco Shells Half Price — Have a Fiesta Tonight!' '

'Have a fiesta tonight?' said Jane.

I nodded. Jane looked teary. 'Come on,' I said, taking her folding chair and carrying it up Oak Street. 'Come on, Jane. Life's a fiesta.'

She smiled, but it was fake. I was her sister, and could tell.

★   ★   ★

Late that afternoon, we returned to town for the Fire Hose Fights. Jane, the younger kids, and I piled into the apartment over Hill's Market to watch the action from the front window. This year, Dennis and their oldest son, Rick, had formed a team. 'We're going to win, Aunt Alice,' Rick, a towering fourteen-year-old and star of the tiny high school's basketball team, had said the night before. 'It's all about leaning *into* the water.'

'Maybe I should try,' said Jake.

Rick let loose a rude laugh, then caught himself and said politely, 'I'm sorry, Uncle Jake. But it's too late to enter.' He didn't say that Jake was out of shape and hated to be cold or uncomfortable in any way. Jane had taught him manners, it seemed.

We opened beers as the teams faced each other along Main Street, readying themselves to be battered by water shooting from a fire hose. Dennis and Rick wore football helmets and pads covered by foul-weather coats and pants. Some wore motorcycle helmets or bulletproof vests.

'I really shouldn't,' commented Jane, taking a large sip of a beer, then putting it aside. Benjamin knocked over a chair and began to wail.

'It never stops,' murmured Jake. I met his gaze and grimaced playfully. Though I'd always wanted children, Jane and Dennis's life did seem hellish. Our lazy days in Austin seemed like a distant, wonderful dream: crossword puzzles, afternoon siestas. But Jake did not wink in response, or smile. His face was nakedly, painfully sad.

'Oh, have another beer,' I told him, annoyed. He shook his head and looked away.

I knew what he wanted from me: sadness equal to his, wallowing, maybe tears. But I was not that sort of woman. I turned my attention from him — he was an adult, after all, and could take care of himself. Though I realized it wasn't fair or even right, I despised him for his weakness. After all, he was the one who had decided to stop trying for a baby! I had told him a thousand times that taking action was the way to move past sorrow. But perhaps everyone needs to learn this lesson for themselves. I'd grown impatient waiting for him to figure it out.

'Ow!' shrieked Gilmer, who seemed to have pulled the bathroom shower curtain down and become entangled.

'Oh my God,' said Jane. She pressed her fingers to her eyes.

'What can I do to help?' I said, settling into a chair to watch as the adult teams turned on their jets.

Jane just sighed.

'Holy Christ!' yelled Jake, looking out at Main Street. 'Rick and Dennis just knocked somebody down!'

'Yahoo!' cried Jane, cheering up, lifting her fist. 'Go, baby!'

Later, we gathered around Jane and Dennis's dining room table for brisket. 'Dad?' said Jane. 'Would you like to say grace?'

'Grace?' I said. 'Since when do we — '

'God, our Heavenly Father,' said my dad, 'we thank you for the food we are about to share. We thank you for our health and our loving family. We ask for your blessings, now and always, and a special blessing for Jane and Dennis's new baby. Amen.'

Jane lifted her face and met my stunned gaze. 'Yup,' she said. Her face was pale, resigned.

'Congratulations, you guys!' said Jake, standing up to hug Jane and Dennis. His words were falsely cheerful, like fluorescent bulbs over a hospital room.

'Wonderful news,' said my father. He repeated, 'Wonderful news.' And then Benjamin knocked over his Kool-Aid and began to cry.

'Look at this smoke ring,' said Dennis, holding up his meat and pointing. 'We're in the hands of a master here.'

'Honey,' said Jane, 'can you get Ben some more Kool-Aid?'

'No,' said Dennis. 'No, I cannot.'

Jane stood up, used her napkin to sop up Benjamin's spilled drink, and then burst into tears.

'Did I tell you guys,' I said, 'that I'm going to help out at the high school?'

'What?' said Jake.

'Yeah,' I said. 'The principal of Chávez Memorial High has asked me to meet with some of the kids. I'm going to mentor a girl named Evian when school starts in the fall. In fact, Evian shot her brother. By mistake.'

Even Gilmer went silent. Jane sank back down in her seat, seemingly relieved to be out of the spotlight. 'Did you say *shot her brother?*' said my father.

'That's what I said.'

'Wow,' said Jake, sounding hurt. 'I didn't know you were going to say yes.'

'The Lord works in mysterious ways,' said my father.

'I guess so,' I said.

'Your mother would be proud of you,' said my father. It was the first time he'd ever said anything like this to me. I stuffed a forkful of beans into my mouth. Happiness rose inside me like bread.

13

Carla

I tried to remember everything I knew about preparing for a trip to America. I made Junior memorize our mother's phone number, starting with the magical Austin, Texas area code, 512. I piled on layers of clothing and strode around our yard, to see if I could take the heat. I practiced tying bottles of water to my waist. I took every *centavo* I had and filled the coffee can, then jammed it deep into my backpack.

'I'm not leaving,' said Junior, sitting cross-legged in the yard.

'Oh yes you are,' I said.

Junior stood. 'See you later,' he said, hitching up his pants.

'Where are you going?'

'None of anybody's business and especially none of yours,' said Junior. I scowled, and he ran off.

'Be back tonight,' I called. I had decided we would leave first thing in the morning. I hoped — dear God, I hoped — that Humberto would join us. I knew it was stupid to try to go to America without a *coyote*, but even with the money my mother had sent that week, we had only thirty U.S. dollars. This was a lot, but it was not enough. When we reached the American border, I hoped it would get all three of us (if Humberto came along) across the Rio Bravo on a raft.

As I've said, I believe in God. I could worry about what I could worry about, and I had to trust God to take care of the rest. As my story continues, please remember this. Some of the things that happened to me would ruin a person who did not have faith. If despair runs as deep and fast as the Rio Bravo, my belief that I am not alone forms a lifeboat underneath me, keeping me from drowning. This is hard for an American to understand. Having enough — having too much — enables you to forget that you are not in charge. God is in charge. But letting go of your fear also means you must accept whatever life God gives to you. I believed, as I prepared for my journey, that God had great plans for me. I saw my reunion with my mother, our picnic lunch, as clearly as I saw the pale sky. I thought this faith gave me strength. Then again, I also believed God would save my brother.

★   ★   ★

So I rummaged through the kitchen, finding the last bits of flour and salt, tying a pillow to my backpack so I could be comfortable until someone took the pillow or I had to leave it behind. To reach The Beast, we had to spend two days hiking through jungle, so I washed our socks and shoes and laid them to dry in the sun.

Humberto stopped by that evening, on his way home from the dump. 'You're not really leaving,' he said, 'are you?'

'I am,' I said. 'Are you coming along?'

'You're crazy,' said Humberto. 'What about me?'

'You're invited,' I said, returning to my preparations. Humberto made a huffing sound and kept walking.

'Don't go without saying goodbye,' he said over his shoulder.

'Okay, I won't,' I said.

My brother had not come home by dark. I lay down on the pallet and closed my eyes. When I opened them, he was next to me, warm and smelling of sweat and glue. I breathed in slowly, trying to calm myself. Having an addict along on my trip to America was a bad thing. But maybe in Austin, Texas, Junior would be different. A younger, sweeter boy. I cried for just a short time.

When Junior woke at dawn, I said, 'Just tell me why, Junior. Why are you sniffing Resistol?'

He looked straight at me, unashamed. 'When I have glue, I'm not hungry,' he said. He reached inside the pocket of his pants. Before he could unscrew his glass bottle, I slapped it from his hands.

'No more,' I said. '*No more.*'

'You can't tell me what to do,' said Junior, his tone attempting bravado.

'Please,' I said.

'Give it to me,' said Junior. 'Give it to me or I'll go get more.'

'You don't have any money!' I said. But then I understood. All I had to do was look to see the empty coffee can on the floor.

14

Alice

In Colorado, you felt fall in your bones — the temperatures dropped, the leaves turned flame-colored, and snow began to accumulate on the mountains. In Texas, fall felt about the same as summer: hot as hell. I could only tell that the school year had begun by the hordes of UT students who arrived at Conroe's, sipping beer through the sweltering mornings. Principal Markson stopped in to celebrate the first day of school with a Sweet Stacy and a lemonade.

'Are you still up for visiting Evian?' she asked.

'Sure,' I said, not feeling sure at all.

'Excellent,' she said, grabbing a Conroe's BBQ pen. She jotted down directions to Evian's house on a napkin using her left hand, not wanting to put down the sandwich she was clutching in her right. (In her defense, the Sweet Stacy *does* fall apart if you loosen your grip; there's a lot of meat jammed into that bun.)

★ ★ ★

The following weekend, I told Jake I wouldn't be able to make our usual Saturday afternoon paddle. He had already laid out picnic ingredients in the kitchen. 'What do you mean?' he said. 'I can't go without you — I need a shuttle. We always canoe on Saturdays!' Jake put down the mayonnaise and crossed his arms.

'I'm sorry,' I said, and I was — I loved our lazy trips. I explained that I'd made plans to meet Evian, the troubled teen.

'Why didn't you tell me earlier?' said Jake, exasperated.

'I guess because I figured you'd act like this,' I said sharply.

'All right, fine,' said Jake, lifting his hands and walking out of the kitchen.

'Hey!' I called. But Jake didn't answer.

★   ★   ★

Though I'd lived in Austin for thirteen years, I had never turned off Oltorf by the train tracks before. I consulted my napkin as I drove.

Turn south on Claiborne. When the road ends, keep going. Evian lives in 3rd trailer on right, though might be running around area. Just ask! Good luck! Watch for dogs.

Watch for dogs? Good Lord. I turned off

Oltorf, ignoring the clumps of grubby folks who gathered underneath the trees, waiting to hop on the next train. At least I assumed they were waiting for a train. Maybe they were just sipping beer in the shade. In a Texas heat wave — it was 112 degrees — all bets were off. Whatever you had to do to stay sane was all right by me. Canoeing was our Saturday pastime, but on Sundays, Jake and I filled the tub with icy water and beer and settled in. It was sort of like relaxing in a pool, I told myself, but without the risk of melanoma.

As promised, Claiborne Street ended, and I drove the Bronco along a dirt road into a ramshackle trailer park. Two large dogs ran toward my truck. One, a German shepherd, barked loudly, exposing a red mouth. Terrified, I hit the automatic locks. I pulled into the driveway next to the third trailer on the left, a tilted structure with empty window boxes. The shades were drawn, and an air-conditioning unit hung outside, humming loudly. At least they had AC, I thought. The big dogs watched me for a few minutes, then retreated.

Uneasily I opened my truck door and the heat slammed into me, a burning steamroller. It was strange to think of the beginning of the school year in Colorado, how we'd worn sweaters and jeans. In Austin, the kids wore shorts and flip-flops into December. I gasped for breath, scorching my lungs, and stood, my thighs peeling off the driver's seat with a revolting sound. I locked the car and plodded torpidly toward Evian's trailer.

I tapped at the metal door but there was no response. I put my hands on my knees, then stood and pounded a bit harder. The door opened, revealing a short black girl with frizzy hair spilling out of a high ponytail. She was plump, her tummy pooching out between a midriff-baring tank top and a pair of neon yellow stretch pants. 'Hi,' I said. 'Are you Evian?' She nodded without smiling. 'I'm Alice,' I said. 'Alice Conroe? Did Principal Markson tell you I'd be coming by?'

The girl nodded again, not taking her big, sad eyes off my face. Despite the AC unit, Evian's trailer was hot, and smelled like cigarettes and corn chips. 'Is your mom here?' I asked.

'She's asleep,' said Evian.

'Oh, okay,' I said. Evian's mother had signed the release forms allowing me to meet with Evian and take her on 'afternoon outings,' but I'd figured she'd want to meet me before I spirited her daughter off. 'Should we wake her?' I said. 'Maybe tell her I'm here?'

Evian shook her head. 'It's fine,' she said in her queer, hoarse voice.

I nodded. The room behind Evian was dim, filled with an overstuffed orange couch and a big TV. Was this where Evian's little brother had died, bleeding into the brown shag rug? I shook off the thought. 'Okay,' I said. 'Well, we can do whatever you're in the mood for. Bowling, or a movie . . . ?'

Evian shrugged. 'I don't care,' she said, looking down.

'I need some clothes, too,' I said. 'We could hit the thrift stores. Or go boot shopping?' As soon as I spoke, I realized how stupid this sounded. Evian likely lived on government cheese and the Bugles I saw spilling out of a bag on the floor. I berated myself: boot shopping! I hadn't even realized how privileged I was until I'd spoken. Evian wore large sneakers without laces or socks. 'I feel like I'd better talk to your mom,' I blurted.

'Okay,' said Evian.

'Can you . . . can you wake her?'

Evian didn't move. 'She doesn't like it if you wake her,' she said finally.

'Oh, of course!' I said, my voice as big and cheery as a circus tent.

'I can do whatever I want,' said Evian. 'She doesn't mind.' This was said with tentative pride. The whole scenario was beginning to depress me beyond measure. And then inspiration struck.

'How about we cook?' I said. 'We can hit HEB down the street, then come back here and make . . . well, what do you like? Brownies?'

'I'm not really interested in cooking,' said Evian politely.

'Oh . . . okay,' I said.

'Can we go to the mall?'

'The mall?' I repeated, dumbly. I was not a fan of malls. I knew Austin had them, and I'd once been to the movies out at Gateway, but something about malls gave me the heebie-jeebies. All that recycled air, the smell of cheap fabric and pretzel bites. 'Sure,' I said, recovering. 'The mall! Why not? Why not the mall?'

Evian slipped past me into the driveway. I followed, unlocking the truck. When dogs ran toward us, Evian quickly clambered into the Bronco, and I did the same. 'Scary animals,' I said after we'd slammed shut the doors.

'They fight them,' said Evian.

'Oh,' I said, locking the car and peering out at the dogs. Who the hell was *they*? 'That's sad,' I noted.

Evian shrugged. 'Wow,' she said, 'this car is like, vintage.'

'I like it,' I admitted. The truth was, I loved it — loved the idea of myself as someone who belonged behind the wheel of a powerful vehicle. The Bronco was a truck even my father admired. I even adored the tape deck and kept a shoebox full of tapes (Van Morrison, Willie Nelson, Wilco, Janet Jackson) between the front seats.

We pulled out of Evian's driveway and headed toward Oltorf Street. 'Are those guys waiting for the train, do you think?' I asked Evian, to make conversation. She shrugged again. 'How old are you?' I tried.

'Fifteen.'

'Oh, fifteen!' I said. I could scarcely remember being fifteen, a ninth-grader at Ouray High. 'How many kids are in ninth grade at Chávez?' I asked.

'Like ten thousand,' said Evian.

'What?'

'I'm joking,' said Evian. 'Who knows? Anyway, we call it Johnson, even though it's *officially* Chávez.' She used her fingers to put quote marks around 'officially.'

'Oh, okay,' I said.

'They fired all our teachers and changed the name, but they can't stop us calling it what we want,' said Evian. She looked at me, eyebrow lifted, challenging me to disagree.

'Right,' I said in solidarity. At a stoplight, I consulted my phone. 'Now, which mall are you interested in?' I asked.

'Barton Creek,' said Evian.

'Great,' I said, getting directions. We headed toward the highway. 'Do you need something specific?' I said. 'Maybe some new . . . earrings? I could use pajamas, actually.' I smiled in her direction, deciding to treat her like a little sister. I could even buy her a pair of earrings. Or some bigger pants . . . or better yet, a flattering sundress!

'I'm meeting my boyfriend,' said Evian.

I was barreling down Lamar and did not know how to respond. I was certain this was not how Principal Markson wanted my afternoon with Evian to unfold. 'Your boyfriend?' I said, trying to sound fun and lighthearted.

Evian picked at her nails.

'So . . . ' I said. 'What's his name?'

'Sam,' said Evian.

'Sam,' I said. 'I don't think I know anyone named Sam.'

Evian was silent, and the awkwardness of my words and the whole damn outing huddled between us like an ugly pet. 'So Principal Markson thought it might be . . . um . . . thought it might be fun for us to hang out this year,' I said.

'Yeah,' said Evian.

Emboldened by this vague affirmation, I went on, 'You could come by my restaurant after school once in a while. We could . . . spend time together.'

'Could you pay me?' she said, turning toward me. 'Like, give me a job?'

'You're not old enough, I don't think,' I said.

'Are you sure?' asked Evian hopefully. 'I need some money. So I can get my own phone and save up for things.'

'What sort of things?' I asked, happy to change the subject from labor laws to hopes and dreams.

'I don't know,' said Evian, putting her floppy sneakers on the dashboard. 'Like a house, you know?'

'A house!' I said. 'I thought you meant clothes. Or, I don't know, an Xbox.'

'I'm not into video games,' said Evian. 'But Sam, he loves them. No, I want to get my own house. I'm going to move to California or New Zealand.'

She spoke so matter-of-factly, I wasn't sure how to respond, other than nodding enthusiastically, Muppet-like. We were zooming along 360, the mall coming up on our right. I concentrated on the road, murmuring, 'I've never been to New Zealand.'

'Me neither,' said Evian. 'Or California. I've never been anywhere except Six Flags once in San Antonio.'

'How was it?' I said, merging into the right-hand lane.

Evian didn't respond. I followed the turn to Barton Creek Mall, passed rows upon rows of parked cars baking in the sun, then finally found an empty slot. I shut off the engine and turned to Evian, which was when I noticed she was crying.

'Evian?' I said, putting my hand on her back. Sweltering air began to seep inside the Bronco.

'I'm fine,' she said, but she leaned toward me. She stopped crying, rubbed her eyes angrily. 'My brother threw up on the Pandemonium,' she said. 'I told my mom he was too little, but she took him on it anyway.'

'Evian . . . ' I repeated.

'You're supposed to be forty-two inches to go on the Pandemonium,' said Evian, looking up at me. I nodded. 'My brother was only *forty* inches. She shouldn't have let him go,' she said. 'It was too scary.'

I paused. Like lobsters in a pot, we began to grow red-faced from the heat, and I wondered whether I should turn the truck back on. Was this what being a parent felt like? Confused, tongue-tied, wishing you had the right words or were somewhere else entirely? My stomach hurt. 'What's the Pandemonium?' I said.

'It's a ride,' she said, annoyance creeping into her tone. 'At Six Flags, in San Antonio.'

My head spun. 'I've never been to Six Flags,' I said.

'My brother's name was Bruce,' said Evian. 'Even though we're black, my mom named him after Bruce Willis.'

I turned the car back on, and air wheezed from the vents.

'He's dead,' said Evian. 'That's why you're taking me to the mall, right?'

'Um,' I said.

'Principal Markson, she told you I killed my brother, right?' said Evian.

I opened my mouth, but did not speak.

'It's okay,' said Evian. 'But you can see why I need a job. In New Zealand, nobody knows about Bruce.'

'I can give you a job,' I said.

'Awesome,' said Evian. 'But can we get going? Sam told me to meet him in front of Foot Locker at two. He's nineteen, so he can't just come and pick me up. He'd be arrested, you know?'

'Uh-huh,' I said noncommittally. Sitting in the mall parking lot, as the car began to cool and the sun beat down on the windshield like a terrible beast, I wrestled to find something to say to Evian. Clearly, I was in over my head.

15

Carla

Needless to say, we did not leave right away for America. The following Wednesday, when my mother called, I asked her for more money. She did not say anything, and then, just when I thought the call had been dropped, she said, 'Carla . . . I'm having a hard time.'

'What is it?' I asked. My throat felt as if I had swallowed coins.

'I don't want to burden you,' she said.

'Mami, what?'

'It's just . . . life is not perfect for me,' she said, her voice as threadbare as Junior's only pair of pants. 'I will do what I can,' she said, in reference to sending money.

I looked at the floor of the Call Shop. It was dirty, covered with a film of the reddish dirt that makes up the hills that enclose Tegu. High in the hills, I had heard, there were rows of stores and sparkling restaurants. Guards with guns stood in front of every beautiful house; unlike us, rich people did not need to rely on cement walls lined with broken glass

98

bottles for protection.

'I will do what I can,' said my mother again.

'Maybe we . . . ' I said, hope a cook fire in my chest, 'maybe we . . . should come to Austin, Texas!'

'No no, Carla,' she replied sharply. 'No, little one. Stay still, and I will save enough for a *coyote*. It will take time, but I . . . I will do it. Children die on The Beast, Carla. Children die and worse.'

Worse? I stood at the Western Union for four hours before a white envelope of *lempiras* arrived. I went to our empty house and waited for my brother, who was sniffing yellow glue and likely passed out somewhere. I waited for morning so I could go to the dump to pick though trash. Worse? I might as well begin with the Resistol myself. But I knew, even then, that I was meant for great things. Anyway, for better things.

How did I know this? Nobody told me so, for sure. But Humberto loved me, and I knew my mother was working hard . . . all for me and Junior. This gave me a sense that I was valuable. I was not garbage, yet somehow my brother was too weak to understand. I had to get him away from this place. But how?

I had a boom box, but its batteries had gone dead long ago. Still, I could play songs in my head, as loud as if they were real. For some reason, the only tape we had was the music of a blind black man named Stevie Wonder. Who knew where this tape had come from? I lay on the pallet with my hands behind my head, and I played 'Isn't She Lovely?' to myself. Stevie Wonder had written this song about his baby daughter. I imagined I had a father who sang to me. I imagined I was an American girl, in a pink bedroom with a bed that had a canopy over it. My father came home from work like the fathers in the movies, carrying a square bag (a briefcase) and singing to me. All I had to do was be lovely, and I would be loved.

Enough of that sentimentality.

I sat up to find I was being watched by a boy I had never seen before. He had a shaved head and a thick black number tattooed on his face, one eye framed. If you know anything about the gangs, you will know what the number was, and you will know why I'm not going to write it down. When that journalist was shot through his eye, it sent a message to us all, and don't think you are safe just because you are in America! This gang had just begun to come to Tegucigalpa at this time. A boy my age with the tattoo was something I had never seen before. I had heard of the gang, though — whispers around the dump.

I knew enough to be afraid. I sat up quickly, reaching under the pallet for the crowbar, ready to fight. 'What do you want?' I said.

'What do *you* want?' he said, leaning back against the door frame of my house, looking insouciant. He pulled his shirt away from his stomach, as if hiding something.

My skin went hot with fear. I had no idea what this boy was doing so far from the city. I wrapped my fingers around my metal weapon.

'I want you to go away,' I said, sounding braver than I felt. He pursed his lips, nodded. He stepped inside the house and shut the door behind him. 'I said to go away,' I repeated, my voice weakening. Was he hiding a gun underneath his shirt?

'Do you have any food?' he said, his eyes scanning the room.

'No,' I said.

'I don't feel very well,' said the boy, and then he slumped to the floor. I jumped up, holding the crowbar high. The boy's shirt fell against his stomach, where it was quickly soaked with blood. 'Don't hit me,' said the boy.

My mind reeled. 'I could kill you right now with this weapon,' I said, 'or you could take me to Austin, Texas.'

'Austin, Texas?' he said, barely able to manage the words.

'Me and my brother. He is sniffing Resistol. I need . . . ' My voice broke.

He met my eyes, nodded slowly. 'I can take you,' he said.

Something let go inside me, a bound coil springing loose. This was it — God's plan for us. I nearly fainted with relief. I had almost stopped believing, to be truthful, and yet here he was: the one God had sent to bring me to my destiny.

'Let me stay here for the night,' he said, his voice delicate but sure. 'In the morning, yes, I will take you to El Norte.'

'Okay,' I said. I filled a cup with water from the jug and knelt next to him.

'No one can know I am here,' he said.

I lifted his shirt. There was a deep cut about two inches long and the boy winced, showing big teeth, as I cleaned it. He made a sound in the back of his throat when I took my grandmother's sewing needle, held it to a match, then punctured the boy's skin and stitched the tear shut. When I was done, his eyelids fell. His skin was ashen. I had no medicine to give him. I hoped he would not die.

I was already on my knees. I prayed, thanking my grandmother, thanking God. I knew if I told Humberto, he would not allow me to go. Was it a stupid idea? Maybe it was. But if we stayed, Junior would be lost forever. And I imagined what it would feel like to reach my mother, to rest against her, to feel someone holding me up.

My brother eventually came home. He jumped when he saw the boy, his face registering something other than dull bliss for the first time in weeks. 'What is this?' he said, terrified.

'We are going to America tomorrow,' I told him. 'This boy will help us.'

Junior's eyes were wide. The number on the boy's face told us that he had done evil things. 'We should run,' said Junior.

'Pack your things,' I said.

'I am not leaving.'

I blinked back tears. 'Mom said she wants us with her, and with Carlos,' I lied. 'She hired this boy to take us to America.'

'Really?' said Junior.

'Yes, really,' I said, nodding.

'I don't believe you,' said Junior, turning from me and reaching inside his pocket for his glue.

'It's true,' said a weak voice. Junior and I whirled around. The boy was sitting up. 'Put down the fucking glue, man,' he said. 'Your mother told me to bring you to America. She paid me well. We leave tomorrow.'

'My mother?' said Junior, not sure if he should trust his hopes.

'Yes, your mother. In Austin, Texas.'

Junior's face lit up as if a bulb had been placed beneath his skin. 'She really sent you?' he said.

'I told you so, and I don't want to repeat myself,' said the boy. 'I'm Ernesto, by the way,' he said.

I asked Ernesto how his stomach felt, and he said to close my fucking mouth about his stomach. 'You — you're going to like it in Texas,' he told my brother.

When Junior grinned, he looked like a child.

16

Alice

From the movie theater bathroom, I furtively dialed Principal Markson, but she did not answer. I listened to her icy voice mail (so this was what she sounded like to itinerant teens, yikes) but did not leave a message. Surely she had bigger problems than my mess of a movie date.

Next I called Jake. 'Where are you, hon?' he asked sleepily.

'I'm at the mall,' I hissed. 'This has gone all wrong, completely wrong.'

'Slow down,' he said. 'What's gone wrong?'

'So I drove to the trailer park,' I said.

'What trailer park?' said Jake. 'I was napping — I'm confused.'

I slumped against the tiled wall. At my feet was a discarded popcorn sleeve. Above the faucet, two young girls applied heavy eye makeup: liquid liner, mascara, glittering eye shadow. I gazed at my own, plain face as I said, 'Remember I couldn't go canoeing because I'm spending the day with Evian, the girl Principal Markson wants me to mentor?'

'Oh, I remember,' said Jake. 'So how's it going?'

'It's a disaster. I'm in the movie theater bathroom. *At the mall!*'

'Oh my God,' said Jake. 'Where *is* the mall, anyway?'

'Out Highway 360,' I said. 'But wait . . . Evian's *in* the movie theater, making out with her boyfriend, and his name is Sam!'

'I see,' said Jake dryly.

'What do I do?' I said. 'Should I split them up? What is my role here?'

'Have you tried Marion?'

'What?'

'Principal Markson? Have you called her?'

'You're on a first-name basis with Principal Markson?' I asked. 'Her name is Marion Markson?'

'Let's stay focused,' said Jake.

'Okay,' I said. The girls had finished painting themselves and had begun to watch me with vague interest, so I went inside a stall and locked the beige metal door. I sat on the toilet. 'I tried Principal Markson,' I said. 'She didn't answer. I just don't know what the right thing is for me to do here.'

'Go watch the movie,' said Jake. 'And when it's over, bring the girl home. What movie, by the way?'

'One of the *Iron Mans*,' I said.

'Oh, dear,' said Jake. 'Totally inappropriate.'

'She's not watching the movie,' I said. 'And Jake . . . this Sam is a senior! Or he must be a repeating senior . . . he's nineteen!'

'Complete disaster,' Jake summarized.

'Yeah,' I said, exhaling.

'It's going to be fine, honey,' said Jake. 'Go enjoy the movie. It's good — I went with Benji to a matinee last week.'

'Okay?' I said, but it was a question.

'You're just supposed to . . . be there, I guess,' said Jake. 'Right?'

'I'm not fond of situations I can't control,' I said.

'That's for damn sure,' said Jake. He started to laugh. 'Are you really in the movie theater bathroom?' he said.

'Grrr,' I said.

'Was that a *growl*?' said Jake. 'You're making me hot, hon.'

'Adios,' I said, cutting the line.

★   ★   ★

I was smiling as I washed my hands, then returned to the theater. It was nice and chilly, and I still had half a cup of Diet Coke. Even better, Evian and Sam had stopped making out and seemed to be engrossed in the movie.

'Hi,' I said cheerily, sliding into my chair.

Neither answered me. Sam was a tall Hispanic boy, skinny and dressed in lime-green shorts and an Abercrombie & Fitch sweatshirt with a hood. He wore black-framed glasses and looked as if he'd walked off the pages of *GQ* magazine. I could see why Evian was smitten. What Sam saw in my underage charge was less apparent. But he'd been thrilled when we found him in front of Foot Locker, grabbing Evian's hand, causing her to flush.

'Um, Alice, you said you needed to do some shopping?' Evian had said. 'I can meet you out front for my ride home.'

'How about we go to the movies?' I'd said.

'Uh . . . ' said Evian, cutting her eyes to Sam.

'I heard the new *Iron Man*'s good,' said Sam, shrugging.

'Great!' I'd said. 'My treat!' And I barreled toward the theater, buying tickets and soda and settling into my gum-covered seat. But as soon as the lights dimmed, Evian ducked toward Sam with a kiss, and before long I was sitting next to a hot and heavy situation. I hadn't actually been in such close proximity to other people tongue-kissing since our tenth-grade campout in Mesa Verde National Park. Flustered, I'd ducked out to call Jake. But now I was back.

* * *

When the movie ended, Evian made another plea for time alone with Sam, and again I demurred, telling her I needed to bring her home. 'My mom doesn't care where I am,' Evian insisted hotly.

'I need to do some things at the restaurant,' I said.

'You have a restaurant?' said Sam.

'Conroe's BBQ,' I said, nodding. The neon lights from a Gap Kids store made our faces pale and yellowish.

'That's right by my house,' said Sam.

'Oh, yeah?' I said.

'I'm going to work there,' said Evian. 'I'm going to be a waitress.'

'Well, we'll see . . . '

'I thought you said yes!' Evian scowled and balled her fists at her sides. But then her anger drained and she sighed histrionically and hung her head. She was so mercurial it was hard to keep up. 'Everybody lies,' she said glumly.

'Well, see you in school,' said Sam, seemingly as confused as I. He leaned in for a smooch, and Evian held on to him tightly, then let go and started walking quickly toward Macy's. (Somewhere past the bed-and-bath section was our exit back into the normal world.)

'Nice to meet you,' I said to Sam awkwardly.

'Okay,' said Sam. 'Bye.' He ambled off, and I hurried to catch up to Evian.

'Slow down,' I said.

'Do you think he loves me?' she asked. 'I mean, real love?'

'I don't know,' I said.

'Me neither,' said Evian wistfully. 'Hey, can you buy me a Cinnabon?'

'Yes,' I said, glad to give her something tangible.

'And a Peanut Butter Cup Chillata?' she said, sidling close.

'Sure,' I said. As I was reaching for my wallet, Evian startled me with a quick, tight embrace. Before I had even registered the hug, it was over, and Evian was pointing to the Cinnabon menu, making her desires known.

17

Carla

I woke before it was light, opening my eyes and squinting until the familiar metal roof came into focus above me. I could hear my brother's breathing. For a moment I questioned leaving Tegucigalpa. I had never slept anywhere other than this pallet. Sure, it was lumpy, but it held the memory of my mother's and grandmother's bodies. I understood this house: how to make the stove light (it was tricky, and took a deft touch), where to store flour away from ants, how often you had to sweep to make a smooth place for your feet.

I turned to Junior. He was fast asleep, his eyelashes fanned across his cheeks. Perhaps he was already too far gone, but if we did not leave, there was only one way his life could proceed. I had seen it happen again and again: the evolution of flesh-and-blood children into dim-witted monsters who cared for nothing but glue.

I thought of my mother. The dream of being next to her, of climbing into her lap

. . . it made me feel light with hope. Resting my head against her chest as she ran her fingers through my hair . . .

'Get up,' I whispered to my brother. 'Wake up. It's time.'

'Is Mom really waiting for us?' whispered Junior.

'Yes,' I said.

He turned and stared at me, our faces inches apart.

'Do you promise?' he asked.

I had never lied to my brother before. I swallowed. 'Yes,' I said, 'I promise.'

He allowed himself a tiny smile, then he sat up and stretched. 'They have ice cream at Texas Chicken,' he said. 'They have a thing where you put a cookie, then ice cream, then whipped cream.'

'Oh, yeah?' I said. He nodded fervently.

★ ★ ★

I had dressed in many layers of clothing the night before, and now I helped Junior do the same. We shouldered our packs, gathered our many water bottles, and walked outside. Ernesto was already awake, hiding behind the bushes smoking a cigarette. He stood as we approached, tossed the cigarette to the ground, and pressed it out with his foot. He touched his injury, testing it gingerly. He needed a disinfectant, but this was the least of our worries. 'Follow me,' said Ernesto.

We passed Humberto's house on the way out of town. I wanted to go inside to say goodbye, but I did not know how. I could only believe we would be together again someday, and keep moving behind Ernesto. You had to follow God's plan when it revealed itself to you, and that was that. I touched the cinder-block wall of Humberto's house, pressed my love inside.

We walked for a very long time, hours, first on dirt roads and then through jungle. It grew very hot and humid; Junior did not complain, but his face was mottled. At one point he pulled the baby-food jar from his pocket. I made a move to take it away, but Ernesto said, 'Leave him.'

I set my jaw and kept going. My feet became blistered, and as we pushed on through jungle, it was hard to see anything before us but unyielding vines and their large, sticky leaves. Bugs whistled in my ears and flew into my eyes and mouth. I was glad Ernesto was with us, as I would not have known in which direction to continue. 'Will we stop for the night?' I said. The pain from my feet was growing raw; I could see blood when I examined my ankles.

'We must reach the river,' said Ernesto.

I stopped maybe two hours after this exchange, sitting down and drinking from a bottle. Junior sank next to me, reaching for the water. Ernesto was ten feet in front of us, and he turned, saying, 'Don't rest! I'm warning you.'

We stood. We continued. It was sunset by the time we reached the river. Despite the misery in my body, I was moved by the sight of the mountains of Guatemala, outlined by cinnamon clouds.

'Take off your clothes,' said Ernesto.

'I will not!' I said.

Ernesto put his face very close to mine. 'Don't be stupid,' he said. 'If you listen to me, we might make it to Texas.' Since my grandmother died, I was not used to taking orders from anyone. Though Ernesto scared me, it was a relief not to be in charge. 'I'm not looking at your chest,' said Ernesto dismissively. This was true. He was staring at the large waves that surged across the river. Maybe he understood how to move through the current, I told myself unconvincingly.

Junior and I stripped to our underwear. (I kept on my shirt. I barely had breasts, though the area around my nipples was hot and a little puffy. Still, I wasn't going to expose myself like a prostitute.) We copied Ernesto's movements, jamming our clothes in our backpacks and holding them overhead as we slid down the side of the riverbank, our feet growing slimy with mud.

Ernesto strode forward, seemingly untouched by the water, which reached my rib cage. Junior cried out, terrified, and I put my arm around him, pulling him alongside me. The water was brown, forceful, smelling of earth. Fear made me strong, even as it made my mouth bitter. My feet lost touch with the ground and I tried to swim forward.

I prayed we would not drown.

'Hold on, Junior!' I screamed. He wrapped his skinny body around my back as I tried to propel myself with my arms and legs. I swam toward the opposite bank, where Ernesto stood on dry land, pulling on his pants. Junior's tight grip pulled me under the waves. I struggled to keep my mouth above water.

'Help me, Ernesto!' I yelled. Junior's flailing arms circled my neck. Ernesto turned around and met my eyes. Then he stepped back into the water and held out his hand. I took it, his grip a solid thing. He pulled us both to safety.

In Guatemala, I lay on the muddy bank, breathing hard. Junior did not release me, but burrowed closer. His backpack was gone. 'Thank you,' I said, looking up. But there was no answer. Ernesto had already begun walking down a brushy path, headed for the next country, which was Mexico.

We stood, and we followed him.

18

Alice

Jake was asleep in his bathing suit when I got home, half an iced tea in front of him on the coffee table, a Yankees game buzzing on the television. The striped towel he took swimming was damp, hung over a chair at the kitchen table. I let myself be still for a minute, watched his chest rise and fall. Jake wasn't *fat*, exactly; he was strong and loved to swim and play touch football. Like his father, Jake had been a star quarterback. His parents' giant brick house in Lockhart (located across the street from the football stadium) was filled with framed pictures of Jake in his Lions uniform, posing with the team.

High school football was a big deal in Lockhart; Jake had once hoped he'd play in college, maybe even pro. But a knee injury had derailed him, leading him to New York, and to me.

I sat next to my husband on the couch, wrapped my arms around his girth. He smelled like sunscreen and chlorinated water. His skin was hot against my face. He had been looking

117

at the *Austin American-Statesman* when he'd fallen asleep, and I narrowed my eyes to see that he'd been reading the classifieds. More specifically, the 'Pets and Livestock' ads.

Jake rolled toward me, murmuring something about a spaceship. I nestled close, then had a crazy idea. Carefully I took the paper from under his arm. I moved quietly to avoid waking him, going back outside into the blazing afternoon.

In front of their house, Camilla watched her children playing in a plastic pool. She wore a tiny string bikini and her skin glistened with oil. She waved lazily. I waved back. 'Come over!' she cried in her lilting accent. 'Is it time for margaritas?'

'Not for me, thanks,' I said, walking across the alley to her house. 'I'm on a mission,' I confided.

'A mission?' said Camilla, sitting up. Her thick black hair fell in a braid down her back, and she wore a wide straw hat. 'Tell me more,' she said. 'This sounds very exciting.'

Her kids splashed each other, somehow energetic despite the heat. 'Jake wants a dog,' I said.

'Oh, no,' she said.

'What do you mean, *oh, no*?' I said.

'Dogs,' said Camilla, tossing her hand as if shooing a fly. 'What about a fish?'

'Can we get a fishy, Mommy?' asked one of Camilla's daughters.

'Absolutely not, no,' said Camilla.

'Awww!' the girls cried.

'I had the strangest day,' I said, sitting on Camilla's front steps.

She made a questioning sound, and I told her all about Evian, Sam, and the movies. I told her about returning Evian to her trailer, where we discovered her mother passed out on the couch, an empty jug of Chablis on the coffee table. 'I didn't want to leave Evian,' I said. 'But she insisted she was fine.'

Sadness flared in me as I remembered the way Evian had stepped quickly in front of her mother, embarrassed. 'She works really hard, so obviously she's super sleepy on the weekends,' Evian had said, ushering me back outside. As I drove away, I saw Evian come outside with the empty wine jug, tossing it in the trash, sinking down onto her front stoop, placing her chin in her hand.

'What you need will come to you, Alice,' said Camilla gently. 'You don't have to go trying so hard.'

'That sounds great, Camilla,' I said, annoyance sour in my stomach. 'But it's not so easy for everyone.'

'I know, I know,' said Camilla. 'But I thought I was meant to be a scientist, and

119

then Beau ran into me with his bicycle.'

'What?'

'It's true,' she said. 'I was visiting Texas for the summer, taking biology classes at UT and also painting and drawing. I set up my easel along Bee Caves Road to paint the bridge at sunset. There I was, beginning to sketch, and a man in spandex biking shorts came along and knocked me over.'

'Beau hit you with his bike?' I said.

'Beau hit me with his bike!' she exclaimed. 'Worse, he sprained his ankle in the fall. You know how he clips his shoes to the pedals? So I had to take him to the hospital. And, well . . . here I am. Sunbathing in a yard with American daughters instead of on a real beach with an ocean. I'll be a U.S. citizen next month.' She sat back, satisfied that she had made her point.

Camilla's daughters began singing a song called 'Party in the USA,' and I stood. 'Well,' I said, 'if I get a puppy, I'll come introduce him.'

'Puppy!' cried Camilla's younger daughter.

'Why not?' I said.

'Well, the dog hair,' noted Camilla.

'Please don't rain on my parade,' I said.

Camilla stood. 'We are not raining on your parade,' she said. And then she added grandly, 'In fact, we will join you on your mission, Alice. Girls, get dressed. We are going to find Alice a dog.'

'I wasn't sure I was going to go right now,' I said.

'Austin Pets Alive! is behind the YMCA,' said Camilla. 'Come on, we'll take my Honda Odyssey.'

'You should put on a dress or something,' I said.

'American prude!' cried Camilla. 'But good point, regardless.'

★　★　★

The girls were apoplectic with excitement as we drove toward the animal shelter. I could never remember which was Ella and which was Bella, so I addressed them in the plural. 'Girls,' I said, turning around to face them, 'I'm not positive we're getting a dog today. I probably need to do some research first. This is just a fact-finding mission.'

'*I love puppies!*' shouted one of them.

'*I love puppies, too!*' screamed the other.

'You're going to have to get the dog right now,' said Camilla. 'I'm sorry, but they'll be too upset if not.'

'Camilla,' I said, 'getting a dog is a big decision. This trip . . . it's a lark. We're just having fun.'

'I hear you,' said Camilla. 'I wouldn't want to clean up the shit of the dog either.'

We parked in front of the shelter. When we exited Camilla's minivan, we could hear the frantic yelping of caged dogs. 'Oh, God,' I murmured, remembering the mongrels that had rushed my car near Evian's house. What the hell was I doing?

'Girls,' said Camilla, 'this is a *no-kill* shelter. Which means if Alice doesn't get a dog today, she can get the dog tomorrow!' She clapped her hands, and the girls nodded seriously.

'You're a great mom,' I said.

'I love it very much,' said Camilla. 'Who knew? This was what I was meant to be, when I thought I was meant to be famous.' She winked. 'Like you and Jake,' she said. I blushed; we had been on the front page of the *Statesman* the week before, and *Bon Appétit* was planning a visit. There was even word of Jake joining the cast of a new reality TV show called *Barbecue This!*

As we ambled toward the shelter, I tried to ignore an acrid smell of urine and ammonia. I pushed open the door to the office, and a genial man with a ponytail greeted us. 'What can we do for you today?' he asked.

'We're just looking around,' I said.

'*We're getting a puppy!*' cried one of the girls.

'Is that right?' said the man, smiling.

'Maybe,' I said. I had begun to regret the entire expedition. Visiting these desperate animals wasn't a *lark*, as I myself had called it. Even if I did adopt one of these abandoned animals, I would leave the rest behind. I felt useless and sad.

'Have a look around,' he said. 'Dogs to your left, cats to your right. You can take any dog you want for a walk. Just let us know.'

As soon as we approached the row of cages, my stomach began to hurt. There were so many of them — bounding toward us, some barking, others sitting very still. The large majority of the animals seemed to be pit bulls. Each had been given a name, and a placard was filled out, describing their personalities. *Charlie is rambunctious and would be happy in an active family with children! Roxanne needs one-on-one atten-tion and will thrive in a childless home!* Young volunteers rinsed bowls and consulted clipboards, nodding as we passed. Classical music played loudly. The girls fell quiet, and I wondered if this place — the enormous need on display — was too much for them. Camilla walked slowly past the dogs, stopping to peer in at each one.

In a far corner, I saw a puppy sitting quietly. He met my gaze and cocked his head.

'Camilla,' I said, grasping her arm.

'Ah, there he is,' she said, following my look and nodding.

I approached the little dog. *Justin Bieber is six weeks old. He's sweet and energetic and needs a forever family!* The puppy was part Bernese mountain dog for sure, but smaller than a purebred. He began to pant, standing up on all fours, but did not bark. I held out my hand, and he came forward, touched his cold nose to my palm. 'Hey, you,' I said. He looked at my face, hope pure and painful in his eyes.

I turned around to see Camilla smiling at me, her arms tight around her girls.

'Oh, boy,' I said.

'Oh, boy,' agreed Camilla.

19

Carla

We spent the first night away from home in a Guatemalan graveyard. I held Junior in my arms as he slept fitfully, gasping once in a while, as if still underwater. Ernesto lay atop another grave, smoking his last cigarettes. We were hungry but expectant: in the morning, we would take buses to the train station in Arriaga, Mexico, where we could climb on top of The Beast. The border crossing between Guatemala and Mexico was dangerous, Ernesto whispered. He had made the journey to America twelve times. (This was his thirteenth.)

His first time, he said, was with his father, who worked picking oranges in Florida. Ernesto hated the groves, hated the tiny motel room shared with twenty men, the way his father drank beer and cursed at him. On rainy days — and sometimes the rain lasted for weeks! — the men watched television all day long, packed into one room, growing agitated. It was terrible, said Ernesto. When I asked him how old he had been during his first year in America, Ernesto gestured toward my sleeping six-year-old brother with his cigarette. 'His age, about,' he said. Still, Ernesto's father had thought him big enough to climb ladders into orange trees, grabbing fruit as fast as he was able, holding a large and heavy sack over his shoulder.

In Florida, Ernesto had missed his mother and sisters, who had remained in Honduras. One night while his father and the other men were out at a nearby cantina, Ernesto ran away. The money he had stolen got him a bus ticket to Los Angeles, where he hoped he could find a family like the ones he saw on his favorite television show, *Beverly Hills, 90210*. But before he reached the state he had dreamed about, someone on the bus reported him as an unaccompanied minor, and he was deported.

Life in his Honduran village no longer fit Ernesto. His mother was strict, and Ernesto bridled at her rules, talking back, even hitting her. Within six months, she hired a *coyote* to bring him back to his father, where he could earn money and be out of her hair. They did not ride The Beast, but traveled by *combi* all the way to the Texas border, where fake papers got him into Laredo and on a bus to Florida.

Upon his return, his father beat him until

he cried, gave him one day in the motel room to recover, then handed him a sack and brought him back to the groves. 'I ran away again,' said Ernesto, 'and this time I reached Los Angeles. It was not, of course, like the television show. But after a bad time, I found my family. My *real* family.'

'Your real family,' I repeated.

It had begun when Ernesto was ten years old, and a boy he thought was a friend carved the words 'El Santa Muerte' into his arm with a sharp knife while other gang members held Ernesto down. Ernesto rolled up his sleeve to show me the crude tattoo. 'I had no choice once I was marked,' he said, gazing at the scar in wonderment. After a moment, he lifted his head. 'But it was all for the best,' he said.

I did not ask him about the gang, about what he had to do to remain in the gang. I did not ask him how he ended up bleeding in my house.

'What will you do now?' I said.

'Whatever God wishes,' said Ernesto. In the light cast by stars, his face was smooth, and I could imagine how handsome he would have been were it not for the number on his face. But then he laughed, a hopeless, strangled sound. 'Or El Santa Muerte,' he said.

I did not mention that I believed in God (and not in the Saint of Death, though her name frightened me). I shut my eyes and said a silent prayer: *Please, God, watch over me. Please bring me safely to my mom.* Before long, I was asleep.

In my dream, I wore a black dress. Humberto stood at my side, also in midnight-colored clothes. I saw my mother, Stefani, and Gabriela. We seemed to be standing at the edge of something, but as I peered down, Humberto said, 'Look up, only up, *mi amor.*'

I defied him. Below us was a grave, a deep earthy hole. At the bottom was a small coffin. One by one, those around me dropped roses on the coffin. 'Goodbye, Junior,' said my mother, and then I understood.

I woke gasping for breath, knowing even as I gazed at my brother's sleeping face that I would lose him. I did not know when or how, but I was sure now that my time with him was limited. I swore to be more vigilant, to keep him next to me no matter who — or what — tried to take him away. Despite my vows, I was filled with the cold knowledge that I would fail.

★ ★ ★

In the morning, we resumed walking, ignoring our bloody ankles. Both Junior and I had good American sneakers, and we had begun the journey with three pairs of clean socks. (Junior's socks had been eaten by the river. I gave him mine.)

Ernesto wore plastic soccer sandals, which looked cool but offered him no support. I thought he was kind of an idiot, if handsome. Around midmorning, we came upon a town, and I opened the coffee can and bought us tortillas, eggs, and cold water. We sat in the shade of a jacaranda tree to eat. 'You need bandages,' commented Ernesto, gesturing to my feet. When I explained that I had no bandages, he pulled my feet into his lap and inspected them. 'Feet, be good,' said Ernesto. Lavender blooms fell from the tree, dusting our hair.

'He loves you,' whispered my brother.

'He talks to feet,' I said. Still, my feet seemed to hurt less as we trekked, leaving the town and heading up a mountainous trail. Junior whined that he was tired, and I reminded him to just put one step after another step. He glared at me, but I thought this was a useful way to think — just keep moving along the path, without worry for what lies ahead or what you've left behind.

Ernesto knew where to board a bus, taking my money to pay our fare. It felt sweet to sit down after walking for so long, to have a moment to feel my brother's head loll on my shoulder, to watch the eucalyptus trees and the verdant fields. ('Verdant' is my favorite English word so far, but I have not yet finished reading *Webster's New Century Dictionary*.) When we entered one small town, a woman climbed on the bus and gave us bread and water for free. 'God bless you,' she said, handing us the food.

It was a new day before Ernesto told us to get off the bus. 'We walk from here,' he said. 'There's a checkpoint ahead.' It was hard to leave the spongy bus seat, and my legs were sore and creaky. Still, we disembarked, leaving the paved road entirely, making our way to a worn trail. We trod along switchbacks as the sun grew fierce, finally reaching what seemed to be the top of something. 'How far are we from Mexico?' I questioned.

'Don't ask,' he answered. He put his hands on his hips, then pointed. In the distance, I could make out another town. 'Tapachula,' said Ernesto, adding, 'Mexico.'

'Will we get there tonight?' said Junior. His voice was a small, cornered animal.

'If you shut up and walk,' said Ernesto.

We shut up. We walked.

★ ★ ★

Ernesto had twice been caught by immigration entering Chiapas. Once he had been robbed. There were a few ways to cross, but Ernesto explained that if we had money, we should hire someone to carry us on a raft. I figured we might as well spend our *lempiras* now, rather than wait to be robbed of them later. The Rio Bravo seemed a world away, and I knew God would provide.

'I have the money,' I said.

Ernesto led us to the Suchiate, a much larger river than we'd crossed before. He bargained with a stumpy man in a baseball cap, then told me to give the man all of my money. I shook my head, and Ernesto stared at me stonily. I saw there was no room for discussion.

'You owe me,' I told Ernesto, reaching into my pack and giving the man the coffee can. Ernesto laughed — that joyless sound again.

The man took us one at a time, Ernesto first. As Junior and I stood on the bank, watching Ernesto cross, I wondered if Ernesto would leave us behind. I told myself we would be fine without him, but I did not believe myself. 'I want to go with you,' said Junior. 'I don't want to be on either side without you.'

I pulled him close. The man returned with the raft and told me to climb aboard. I explained that Junior and I wanted to cross together. The man refused. 'Take him first, then,' I said.

'You don't want him alone with that one,' said the man.

'He's not what you think,' I said.

'Look at his face,' said the man.

I sighed and stepped on the raft. Junior burst into tears, and I implored him to have faith. The raft was unsteady, and despite my words, I was nervous as it rocked back and forth. The man had a long pole to grip the mud below. 'I know what I am doing,' he told me. 'There are alligators in the water, by the way.'

When we reached the other side, I stepped into Mexico. I had left all my papers behind so that if I was caught now, I would not be sent home. I sat down cross-legged and watched as the man returned for Junior. I held my breath. My brother climbed aboard nervously, slowly. The raft leaned to the side but righted itself. In a matter of minutes, Junior was in my arms. Ernesto stood behind us as Junior and I embraced. 'Now the train,' said Ernesto.

'Now The Beast,' said Junior with excitement.

'Now The Beast,' agreed Ernesto. He did not smile.

20

Alice

Jake was still asleep when I got home with Pete. (I'd quickly changed the pup's name from Justin Bieber to Pete, after Pete's Candy Store, the Brooklyn bar where Jake and I had shared our first beers.) Camilla and the girls stood at our doorway with their hands at their mouths, and I set my little guy down and watched him approach my big guy. Pete sniffed the floor. I am embarrassed to say I wondered, in that moment, if he could smell the longing that had permeated our house, perhaps the last traces of the bottle of baby formula that Jake had mixed in the middle of the night, spilling a bit on the floor. I wondered if Pete would want to stay with us on Mildred Street, if anyone ever would stay. But he lifted his head and ran to the couch, springing up and jamming his snout under Jake's wrist, looking for a scratch.

Jake jerked awake. 'What?' he said.

'Surprise!' I cried, and Ella and Bella chimed in, 'Surprise!'

'Am I dreaming?' asked Jake.

I shook my head, stupidly bursting into tears. 'It's Pete,' I managed. 'He's ours. Pete, after Pete's Candy Store.'

'Oh my God,' said Jake, pulling the dog onto his lap and leaning down. Cradling the dog, it must be said, like a child. 'Hey, buddy,' he said. 'Hey, buddy!' Pete barked and licked Jake's face. 'Where did you come from?' asked Jake.

'I adopted him,' I said.

'At the *no-kill shelter!*' cried Ella (or maybe Bella).

'Congratulations on your new arrival,' said Camilla. 'It's time for us to go have supper now. Ciao, Pete. Say ciao, girls.'

The girls said goodbye and waved, complaining as their mother dragged them away.

Jake was beaming. 'He's so awesome,' he said. 'I mean, come on! He's perfect. Part Bernese mountain dog, right? And part . . . ?'

'Who knows?' I said.

'He's ours,' said Jake, but it sounded like a question.

'Yes.'

'Oh my God,' said Jake again. 'We've got to take him for a walk! We've got to buy dog food! We need a bowl, and a dog bed, honey! Where's he going to sleep?'

I shook my head, laughter spilling from my mouth.

Pete jumped to the floor, and Jake picked me up, spun me around. 'I love you!' he said. 'I love my dog!'

I held on to Jake. He was so warm and so alive. And then we headed (with Pete) to the pet store.

★　★　★

That night, as Jake paged through *The Art of Raising a Puppy* by the monks of New Skete (recommended by the clerk at Book People as the best guide around) and Pete sniffed out his new crate, I checked my messages. Principal Markson had called, telling me that she'd stopped by the Claiborne Street trailer and Evian's mom had raved about the wonderful afternoon Evian and I had shared. I thought this was odd, as I'd never even met Evian's mother — she'd been asleep when I picked Evian up and asleep when I dropped her off at home. Principal Markson said she hoped my afternoon outings with Evian could continue. Did next week at the same time work for me?

'Ugh,' I said to Jake. 'I'm just not sure about this. Evian's headed for trouble.'

'You know,' said Jake, who was lying on the floor next to the crate, rubbing Pete's ears through the bars, 'I think I always wanted a dog more than a kid, in the end. I mean, this is fucking awesome.'

'I think the crate is supposed to be his space,' I said. 'In other words, don't go poking your hands in.'

'Oh,' he said, looking chagrined.

'I'm glad you're happy,' I said.

'You're right,' he said, leafing through our book. 'The monks do say not to stick your fingers in the crate.'

'Jake,' I said.

He looked up.

'I . . . ' I said. 'I . . . '

'You what?'

I swallowed my sadness, my feeling that something was missing. After all, we had so much.

'Please, Alice,' said Jake. He stood, then wrapped me in his arms. I started to cry, for the loss of Mitchell, for the baby no dog could ever replace. I didn't mean to be selfish, to ask for more than anyone deserved. But I had a hole in me, and worse: a persistent feeling that someone was looking for me, someone who needed me desperately.

'Please,' whispered Jake, holding me so tight I could feel his heart thumping. 'Please, honey,' asked my husband, 'can't this be enough?'

My cell phone rang early in the morning, yanking me from sleep. Jake had already gone to work; he'd fed and walked Pete beforehand, and Pete was napping in his crate. I fumbled with the phone, stammering, 'Hello?'

'Um, Alice?' said a young voice.

'Evian? This is Evian?' I said.

'Yeah, it's me.'

'Shouldn't you be at school?' I narrowed my eyes and checked the clock: 8:03.

'I was wondering . . . ' Her voice trailed off.

'What?' I said, somewhat impatiently.

'I am at school,' she said. 'Don't be mad. I'm here, I just . . . my mom was kind of wonked out this morning. I wondered if you could maybe . . . check on her. Just make sure she gets up and goes to work?'

I bit my tongue, not sure how to respond. Clearly, this whole Big Sister situation was going to be more than I had bargained for. 'I don't know what to say,' was all I could manage to say.

'Never mind,' said Evian. 'Just forget it. I'll go home and check on her myself.'

'No . . . ' I said. There was silence on the line; she waited.

'Did you say something?' said Evian, when I didn't finish.

'I'll run by,' I said.

'Oh my God, thank you!' said Evian. 'You're totally awesome. Awesome *sauce*, as Sam says. I have, um . . . PE, and I don't want to miss it. You can just text me and let me know? Thanks so much, Alice!' She cut the line before I could reply.

My awkward stammerings had waked Pete. He yipped and pawed at the crate. I let him outside and sat on the porch swing to consider my next move. Coffee, I decided, then Evian's trailer park. I'd pretend I was stopping by to say hello, to meet Evian's mom in person, and then I'd leave. I would text with the news that Evian's mother was fine and dandy and get on with my day. Pete peed in the yard and then crumpled next to me. He peered up, as if to say, *Come on. This heat — it's too much.*

'You're right,' I said, grabbing the brand-new leather leash Jake had picked out and clipping it onto Pete's matching collar. I led him to the truck, opened the hatchback, and laughed as he jumped inside the car and made his way to the front, settling himself on the passenger seat. Again, he glanced back at me with his haughty expression.

'Onward,' I said. I could swear the dog nodded.

Cenote was a gorgeous coffee shop in the

neighborhood, housed in a historic building. Jake and I had watched the progress of the space from an abandoned home (formerly owned by a long-leaf-pine salesman, hence the refinished floors) to an elegant café with robin's-egg-blue walls and large glass doors painted with gold. Jake and I didn't know the owners, but I hoped we'd meet them one of these days. Pete strode alongside me as I approached the counter. I ordered coffee from a swanlike woman wearing a ruby-colored (or maybe actual ruby) stud in her nose.

'Cute dog,' said the woman.

'Thanks,' I said.

'There's water in a bowl outside,' she said, gesturing to Pete, who was panting.

'Oh!' I said, grabbing my coffee and leading him to drink. I had a lot to learn.

Back in the car, I drove west, turning onto the dead-end street where Evian lived. I sipped my dark brew and parked. There was no sign of life inside the trailer, but what had I expected? A motherly woman mowing the lawn or reading a romance novel on the front porch? There wasn't a porch, anyway, just two metal chairs and a rusted coffee can filled with gravel and cigarette butts. And the awful dogs, surrounding my car and barking. Pete barked back, becoming hysterical and pawing the door. Jesus H. Christ.

I did know I couldn't leave Pete in a hot car, so I blasted the AC and got out, trying to ignore the canine mayhem. I rapped on the trailer door and called, 'Hello? Mrs. Kenman?' There was no response. I turned to Pete, met his beseeching gaze through the windshield, and called out for Evian's mother once more. Then I tested the door. It was unlocked. I hesitated for just a moment before stepping across the threshold and saying, 'Hello? Is anyone home?'

Miserably I wandered around the trailer. A cockroach scurried across the kitchen counter, and the master bedroom — the only bedroom — had a hamster in a cage, but there was no human in the place. Not in the bathroom that smelled of mildew and perfume, not in the backyard, not in the corner of the living room that looked like Evian's sleeping quarters. (A blanket, empty Big Mac container, and radio with headphones marked her territory.) I even checked underneath the bed, but, mercifully, no one was there. So I walked back outside, closed the door behind me, got into my car, and drove away. At the stop sign on Oltorf, I texted Evian that her mom wasn't home. I shut off my cell. Pete didn't stop barking until we had reached Mildred Street.

21

Carla

I do not need to elucidate for you the misery of hiking across a desert, so I will not do so. I will say that it was very hot, hotter than you can imagine, and that we ran out of water. I will say that when you are desperately thirsty, there is nothing else in your mind besides want — want of water, want of sleep. Your blood thickens; you grow weak. But enough: we did not lie down.

Eventually we came upon a small village and Ernesto went into a grocery, telling us to keep moving. He caught up with us minutes later, his pockets bulging with stolen items. Ernesto gave me water. He gave Junior water. I loved him.

Ernesto told us that this area — Chiapas — was full of bad people. (This from a boy with pants full of stolen mangoes!) 'They are not all devils,' he said, 'but many are evil.'

'What do you mean, *evil*?' I asked.

He merely shook his head. 'You do not want to know what people can be like,' he said quietly. 'Depraved. Please pray for God to watch over us at this point.'

I did as Ernesto had requested. As we walked through farms, small towns, then larger towns, I gripped my brother's hand and prayed. I understand now that many never make it across Chiapas. At night, sometimes, I read their stories on the Internet, my eyes filled with tears — stories about trafficking, about human slavery, about children trading sex for one square meal. Murder, decapitation, prostitution, gang initiation. I was so lucky.

God was with us: we made it to the train station in Arriaga. If we had not had Ernesto showing us where to go and God keeping us safe, we would have been lost.

It was very late at night by the time we arrived. Ernesto told us to stay still and disappeared, telling us he would try to find out when the next train would be leaving. Junior and I huddled together, trying to make ourselves invisible. I touched the steel train tracks and my hand came away smelling like a burned pan.

Here, in a dark station filled with desperate immigrants, the mood was forbidding. I felt like a dying animal being watched by patient vultures. Everyone was either competing for a place on the train or trying to figure out how to take advantage of us travelers. I could not get enough air in my lungs, and my mouth tasted sour.

'Will he come back?' said Junior.

'Of course,' I said. 'Mami sent him to watch over us.'

Junior buried his nose in his baby-food jar, but there were no fumes left for him to savor. 'I want Mami,' he said. 'What does she look like, Carla?' I felt hollow inside, realizing that Junior didn't even have a memory of our mother's face to sustain him. I knew the way she looked at me, and how her hands felt on my skin.

'She looks like you,' I said.

Junior bit his lip and nodded, wanting to believe me.

My stomach twisted, growling for food, but we had no more money. I was not sure that Ernesto would return: perhaps he had been running from something and now was on safer ground. I saw members of his gang around the station, smoking, speaking too loudly, looking for trouble or opportunity. A few hours passed.

'I want Resistol,' said my brother.

'Don't be weak,' I spat.

'I don't care,' said Junior. 'I want it. I don't care about the rest.'

I put my arms around him, my nose to the top of his head, which smelled like river water. 'Please care,' I said, both to him and to God. 'I'm taking you to a better place, Junior, to Mami.'

He stayed with me. I was thankful.

Finally I saw Ernesto's scrawny figure loping toward us. He held his shoulders back and his chin was lifted. 'Hello, my young friends!' he shouted.

He came closer, reeking of marijuana smoke. He handed us drinks and tortillas filled with meat. My mouth exploded with pleasure at the salty, rich taste of the stew. I almost choked, I ate so fast. As the food reached my stomach, warmth flooded my arms and legs.

'The train is leaving soon,' he promised. 'When The Beast slows, you must do as I tell you.' We nodded. The tracks were swarming with men who would be looking for a place on the train. There were few women, and I could not see another girl. Making it to the top of a car was very important, Ernesto told us.

'Your friends are here?' I asked him.

'My friends are everywhere,' he said proudly. 'You don't have to worry anymore.'

This was the appeal of the gangs — if you obeyed them, they were your family. It is easy to think that people like Ernesto joined gangs to get drugs or food, but in my experience, it was for love.

After about an hour, the train approached, belching smoke. Its brakes shrieked so loud it felt as if someone was plunging a pencil into my ears. 'Go!' shouted Ernesto. Joining the flood of people, Junior and I rushed toward the train. It did not stop, just slowed as it passed through Arriaga, and we ran alongside, trying to get the courage to jump. Ernesto had told us that we should reach for a ladder toward the front of a car, so that if we missed and our feet fell on the rails, we would have an instant to lift them before the wheels ate them up or dragged us underneath.

As I neared the train, it shot hot sparks at me, burning my skin. The lowest ladder rail was above my waist. Ernesto leapt, and I understood this was my chance.

Adrenaline ignited my arms; I grabbed the ladder with all my strength, pulling up, reaching for the higher rung, my feet flailing desperately. But then I found the bar, and I was aboard.

Below me, Junior ran alongside the train. 'Come on!' I yelled, clinging to the ladder. He grasped for and then caught the bottom rung of a boxcar behind me.

'Help me!' he said. He was sobbing, and the air rushing underneath the train began to pull his legs under.

'Don't let go!' yelled a man.

'Heave yourself up, boy!' screamed another.

'Help me!' cried my brother. 'Please, God, help me!' A group of strangers scrambled toward Junior. They reached down, risking their own lives, and wrenched him slowly aboard. He collapsed, and I climbed the boxcar I had boarded. Our journey on The Beast had begun.

22

Alice

'You just let yourself into the trailer?' said Jake.

'It was unlocked,' I said.

He turned to me, his features dark with anger. I'd thought the story was morbidly funny, but Jake seemed angry. 'Well, Evian asked me to check on her mom,' I said. 'She needed me. I just . . . I thought it was the right thing to do.'

'You thought it was the right thing to do?' asked Jake. 'To drive over to a strange neighborhood and wander into someone else's house?'

'Well, yeah,' I said. 'And it's not really a *strange* neighborhood as much as a *menacing* one.'

Jake shook his head. He was having none of my feeble jokes. 'So was the mom there?' he asked.

'No,' I said. 'No one was there. It was really dirty, Jake. It was sad.'

'Poor girl,' said Jake. It was early evening as we walked with Pete along Lady Bird Lake.

147

Pete was thrilled about every single item we encountered, sniffing babies in strollers, weedy plants, and piles of shit without discrimination. I reached for Jake's hand, but his arms were folded over his chest.

'What's the matter?' I said.

Jake stopped abruptly, causing hikers and bikers to swerve around him. He turned to me. 'Alice,' he said, 'I'm worried about you.'

'Oh, really?' I said. An old defiance rose in me, the same emotion I'd felt when my high school counselor had tried to pry into my feelings about my mom's death and when my dad had brought home a nanny to take care of Jane. 'I'm fine,' I said, as I'd said when I canceled sessions with the counselor, and when I'd convinced my father to let the nanny go. 'I am,' I told Jake. 'Truly.'

'Look, we're both struggling,' said Jake. I breathed evenly, waiting for him to stop talking. 'I'll be honest,' he said. 'I'm having a hard time, too. But I'm afraid that you're . . . misplacing your love. You know? You want someone to take care of, but this might not be the right person.'

'Oh?' I said. 'Then who *is* the right person?'

My husband stood before me, opened his arms. If I had looked at his face, maybe I would have understood. Instead, I stared at the lake. It shimmered in the evening light, moving slowly, seemingly untroubled by the dozens of pleasure boats it buoyed.

★ ★ ★

Later that night, my phone rang while we were watching *House Hunters International*.

I glanced at the Caller ID. 'It's Evian,' I said.

Jake shrugged, annoyed. I didn't answer the phone. The couple on the television looked at a modern Croatian house on the outskirts of town and a historic one near a bustling plaza. Neither house had enough closet space. Jake said, 'Go on, listen to the message.'

I picked up my phone. There was no message. The couple on the television looked at a third house, situated on a hilltop with a fabulous view and totally enough closet space but kind of far away from restaurants.

I held my phone like a grenade. I bit my lip. After the commercial break, the couple chose the hilltop home. They were well on their way to a bright future in their new home, Zagreb! Three months later, the couple had furnished the living room and filled the closets. They chopped vegetables side by side and toasted their fabulous view. The credits rolled.

'I don't know why I love that show, but I love that show,' I said.

'I prefer *Pawn Stars*,' said Jake.

'I know,' I said.

Jake stood and stretched. 'I'm going to hit the hay,' he said. 'The *Bon Appétit* reporter arrives tomorrow.' I smiled. A profile in *Bon Appétit* was thrilling.

'I'm so proud of you,' I said.

'You're in the story, too,' said Jake.

'Really?' I said.

'I am pretty happy,' said Jake. 'I mean, holy shit, *Bon Appétit!*'

'I know,' I said. Jake kissed my forehead and headed into the bedroom. I tried to read an old *New Yorker* but couldn't seem to focus. I cared about jalapeño peppers, but not enough to read a ten-page treatise. I read that issue's short story, 'Robbers and Lightning,' which was translated from Korean and left me confused. I went out back, but there were no lights on at Beau and Camilla's. I felt sorry about Evian, not sure if I should call her back or not. Finally I sent a text: *Evian, I saw you called. Hope all is well?*

A few seconds later, she wrote: *I'm OK. Thanks for caring haha.*

I wondered what 'haha' meant in this situation. I was still new to text messaging, baffled by winky emoticons and weird phonetic spellings of sounds. Did 'haha' mean she was feeling happy, or was she commenting ironically on the fact that I wasn't actually caring enough? Was she saying, *Thanks for caring*, then adding a giggle, or was she saying, *Thanks for 'caring,'* and adding a derisive snort?

Jake was right: I wanted to love someone, but Evian wasn't the one I should love. I was sorry for her, but couldn't figure out how I fit into this messy mosaic. I went outside, lay on the lawn, and watched an enormous number of bugs swarming around a streetlamp. A siren wailed. I went back inside and finished reading the article about jalapeños.

23

Carla

Ernesto found us huddled on the boxcar and explained that we should move to a safer location. Boxcars are tall, he said, so we could see *la migra* coming, but they offered little to hold on to. As the train lurched from side to side, gaining speed, the cars sometimes smashed into each other, jarring my head back on my neck. I could see why we needed another perch. People cowered under cars, on ledges only a foot wide, between the axles, on top of round compressors. 'Inside the boxcar seems smart,' said Ernesto, 'but if they close the door, you die of heat. I've seen it.'

Weak and very tired, we followed Ernesto to the top of a hopper, clutching the thin bar along the edge as tightly as we were able with our numb fingers.

The train was moving quickly now. I shouted with fear and excitement, crammed next to men who smelled of sweat, looking out over a sea of treetops. We were on our way! Then, as quickly as the wave of exhilaration had come, it dissipated, leaving me limp. Still, I clasped the rail with one hand and the waistband of my brother's pants with the other. I knew what would happen if I weakened my hold.

As the train rumbled through the night, some played cards and some talked. Some smoked, and some watched the wide sky. If you slept, you put yourself at risk. Ernesto showed us how to attach our belts to the edge so we would not fall. Through the hour, we rode, tree branches whistling overhead. We watched for police (they approached at many stations, raiding the trains), and we watched for gangs, who climbed aboard to rob us. The wind reached underneath my hair to touch my scalp. Junior fell asleep; I kept my hand on him.

I was half asleep when I heard the shouting. I sat up in the dark to see a group of robbers in hooded sweatshirts, showing guns. They yelled, 'Give us money! Give us everything!' I heard an awful cry and saw a man fall, pushed off the top of the train. He hit the ground with his hands at his temples. The train kept moving.

I had no money; I bent down, hoping not to be seen. I felt Ernesto's body on one side of me, immobile. When I cut my eyes to his face, his gaze locked with mine. I could see he was scared. I clasped my brother's pants tightly.

The robbers came closer. I heard the sound of metal hitting bone as they slammed a gun into a man's head. I heard sobbing. And then a robber's legs were in front of me, filthy denim an inch from my nose. A hand grabbed my chin and lifted my face heavenward. I stared into the face of an evil man. His eyes were deep gray, ice: an animal's eyes. 'Beautiful,' he said. I tried to breathe slowly, quietly. Tears ran down my cheeks.

'Lie down,' the man said. I shook my head, pulled it from his grasp. He tore some of my hair from my scalp; his grip was that tight.

'Please,' I managed.

He pushed me flat and climbed on top of me. I sobbed, and he hit me with his fist, then with his gun. I tasted blood. I could not stop shuddering.

I was surrounded by people. A hundred men, some women, my brother, Ernesto. No one did anything as the man pulled my pants down. No one intervened — not even God — as the man freed himself and entered me, tearing a wound. I bit deep into the meat of my tongue. He raped me. When he was finished, he stood up and spit in my face, calling me a whore. He fired his gun into the sky, and when the train slowed, he jumped off and ran away.

No one said anything as the train rushed forward. Not even my brother touched me.

In this way, I understood I was alone.

24

Alice

Visiting Lockhart — BBQ capital of Texas, Jake's hometown, and site of our over-the-top wedding — was awkward under normal conditions, though I'd finally adjusted to the weird dynamics of holiday gatherings. But barreling into town with a *Bon Appétit* writer riding shotgun in my Bronco (Jake drove; Pete and I were crammed in the back) made my stomach ache. The taco I'd eaten for breakfast felt like a hot balloon in my gut.

Lainey, the reporter, had spent the night with my husband, watching him tend the fires at Conroe's and recording his every word. She was sharp-eyed, younger than me, and dressed in flowing layers that would have made me look like a bag lady but on Lainey seemed fashionable.

Lainey smoked Marlboro Reds, which lent her voice a raspy quality. I felt as if we might have been friends had she not been interviewing Jake for an article, thus making it impossible for us to speak normally. Around Lainey, Jake had a bit more of a

Texas twang than usual, pausing for a while between sentences as if practicing them first in his head. I tended to say things very quickly and in a high-pitched voice, concluding with 'You know?'

The drive to Lockhart took about forty-five minutes. For the first twenty, Jake had been clarifying terms. A 'sugar cookie' was the caramelized edge of the meat, a sublime bite of salt and fat. The 'bark' was the black crust; Jake wrapped the brisket in butcher paper as soon as it came off the smoker to preserve every inch. And the 'smoke ring' — Christ, Jake could talk for an hour about that reddish-pink line, the pit master's holy grail, a chemical reaction that occurred when the perfect moisture level in the meat was sustained at the perfect (low) temperature.

'So essentially, the meat is basting itself,' said Lainey rapturously. She turned to me. 'It's impossible, how juicy his meat is. It's . . . transcendental.' She turned her worshipful gaze back to Jake, who looked pleased. I was not sure how to respond to this statement.

'Yup,' I managed.

'He just keeps that fire at such a consistent temperature,' Lainey mused. 'The collagen and fat break down in the meat, and Jake just watches the fire, moving the wood, gauging the smoke. All night, he keeps the temperature low, letting that wet goodness soak in . . . '

'Low and slow,' drawled Jake, 'that's how we do it.' I wondered if, in his imagination, he was the star of some porn project. I saw him peek at his own face in the rearview mirror as he repeated, 'Looow and slooow.' He was not an arrogant man; it was actually pretty wonderful to watch him bask in well-deserved attention. God, I loved him.

'His meat sure is moist,' I voiced.

'Like . . . a dishrag, but that's not the right word,' Lainey continued. 'Like a . . . '

Jake and I waited, expectant. She was the writer, after all.

'A sponge?' she said questioningly.

'There doesn't have to be a metaphor,' I said.

'The point is, if the heat's too high, the brisket wrings out all its water. Hence the need for sauce,' noted Jake. Jake prided himself on not needing any sauce to hide imperfections or dryness.

'But you serve sauce,' said Lainey. 'Now, I know your father doesn't allow sauce,' she said impishly. 'But you and your uncle . . . '

Oh, now she was getting into it, hinting at Jake's famous family feud. I saw his shoulders tense and his brow furrow, and Lainey must have noticed, for she deftly changed the subject. 'We'll get back into the *sauce* later,' she said suggestively. Jake loosened, and they chuckled together. I sighed. Lainey hooked her left arm around the seat and angled her microphone toward me, in the back. 'What was it like the first time you visited Lockhart, Alice?' she asked.

'It was something,' I said, unsure of how to describe the utter dislocation I'd felt upon arriving in Texas. For one thing, it was hard for me to understand how seriously people took barbecue. In Colorado, we sometimes had sloppy joes (hamburger mixed with a packet of seasoning and served on a white-bread bun), and we grilled hot dogs on occasion, and of course venison or whatever my dad shot. I'm sure the nearby ski town, Telluride, had serious barbecue — they had sushi flown in daily, for God's sake — but in Ouray we used a Weber grill, some charcoal with lighter fluid, a match, and maybe a bottle of Heinz 57. How different, I'd wondered when I first visited Jake's family, could 'real barbecue' be?

Our first stop in Lockhart had been Jake's family's restaurant. Harrison's BBQ was housed in a brick building located right on the town square. We parked the U-Haul with all our belongings in front of the Caldwell

159

County Courthouse, a looming limestone structure with a four-way clock reaching toward the blue Texas sky, a clock that reminded me of the one in Grand Central Station. Jake climbed out and stretched — we'd stayed in New Orleans the night before, and had been driving for eight hours. He pointed to Raymond's Barbershop, where he'd had his first haircut. Jake waved to the elderly barber waiting for a customer. We passed the Ruiz Dance Studio. 'Never seen that before,' said Jake, peering into the jam-packed room, where a Zumba class was under way, pouring waves of salsa beats into Main Street.

You entered Harrison's BBQ through a dark doorway, walking down a hall stained black from decades of barbecue smoke. If you peered into a display case on your right (as I had), you'd see pictures of Jake's family over the generations. The smell of rich smoke grew stronger as you approached the pits, brick behemoths with steel tops and wood fires burning hot, feeding smoke to the meat. Piles of oak lay next to crates of Big Red. (Across the street was an entire lot filled with stacked wood.)

You placed your order, then took the hot meat wrapped in butcher paper into a bright, large room filled with long tables and folding chairs. The place was packed with locals and 'barbecue tourists' from 10:00 a.m. until closing, as it had been for decades.

★   ★   ★

'Alice?' prompted Lainey.

'Oh, Lockhart!' I screeched. 'It's really beautiful there, and I was so happy to meet Jake's family, they're just so great, you know?'

My words appeared in my mind in an elegant font: *They're just so great, you know?* I grimaced. Lainey looked at me, unblinking. Surely she knew the story of Jake's family, which was a long and bitter one.

Harrison's had been established as a grocery store along the Chisholm Trail in 1900 by Jake's great-great-grandfather Harrison Conroe. It stayed in the family, eventually transforming into a BBQ restaurant. (The grocery still existed but sold mainly Harrison's caps and T-shirts . . . and beer to go with the BBQ.)

Over the years, various relatives sold their shares, or weren't interested in the day-to-day smoking and serving. By the late 1960s, the restaurant was run by Jake's grandfather. When he died, he left Harrison's to his wife, with plans that she (in due time) would leave the business to their two sons — Jake's father,

Collin, and his brother, Martin.

But then Jake's mother, Winifred, entered the picture, and all hell broke loose.

When he was in his late twenties, Jake's uncle, Martin, met an actual beauty queen (Miss Baytown, 1968) while on a beach vacation. Smitten, he asked her to marry him and brought her home to meet the family. But when the beautiful brunette met Jake's father at her own engagement party, she fell in love with *him* and they eloped to San Antonio that very night. Collin was back at work on Monday with a wedding ring and a stunned smile, and the story goes that when he walked in the door, Martin took a hot brisket right off the rack and threw it at Collin, knocking him flat.

Martin never forgave Jake's father for stealing Winifred. Martin and Collin's mother, Nanette, declared that Winifred was 'bad news from Baytown,' and sold Harrison's BBQ to the bank, giving half the money to Martin, who bought a giant building on the outskirts of town and opened a competing BBQ restaurant, the Lone Wolf. There was a front-page news story on the day Martin dragged a tub of hot, historic coals from Harrison's BBQ down Main Street to fill the state-of-the-art pits at the Lone Wolf. Martin took out advertisements and bought billboards, hired the pit master away from Collin, and built a BBQ empire that eclipsed Harrison's completely.

Then Martin's son, Jeremy, had opened Lone Wolf franchises in Las Vegas, JFK Airport, and Dubai, and we had opened Conroe's Austin. As the barbecue editor of *Texas Meats and Sides* had noted, 'Were it not for family hatred, there would only be one Harrison's BBQ, on Lockhart's town square.'

'So you have a close relationship with Jake's family?' said Lainey innocently. 'And Jake's uncle, Martin . . . you hang out with him?'

'Yes, absolutely,' I said.

'So you all spend time together?' said Lainey. 'Like, when was the last time you were all in the same place?' Lainey was good. Her face impassive, she watched me and waited. I could see Jake's hands tightening on the wheel.

In truth, I had a complicated relationship with Jake's parents. His father lifted weights, jogged every morning, and drank a bit too much. Collin was comfortable with his small-town fame, both as a former football star and as a current restaurateur. This is not to say he didn't work hard — smoking meat is backbreaking, and Collin had been tending the fires since he was a kid. Though he had a staff now, he was still usually at Harrison's at midnight to put the meat in the pits, his hands red with spices, his face flush with his first few beers of the night.

When I had first met Jake's glamorous mother, Winifred, I had adored her completely, enthralled as only a motherless girl could be. She seemed a character out of a movie, with her subtle makeup and the long hair she set each night in curlers. She knew how to hunt and fly-fish and throw large dinner parties on a dime, inviting local bigwigs and her manicurist to the same fête, building a bonfire in the backyard herself, then emerging in vintage couture to stand by the flames holding a cocktail (in one of her highball glasses painted with safari animals — she and Collin had celebrated their thirtieth anniversary with a trip to Kenya) and tossing her tresses over her shoulder as she laughed.

Jake was her only child, and she seemed skeptical of me, but my blind adoration of her must have been appealing. She planned and executed a gorgeous wedding in their backyard, charming all my relatives and giving a heartfelt toast to our happiness.

As it turned out, however, there were many things that were not discussed in Jake's family. The restaurant was bankrupt, for one thing, and Collin was too proud to ask his increasingly rich brother for help. Jake had not told his parents that I was infertile, or that I had been sick at all. These issues had come up during a terrible dinner I had not attended: Jake had gone to his parents to ask them for money for an adoption. They were stunned at my infertility, and he was saddened by their disastrous financial state. Jake came home to Austin and lay next to me in bed, telling me about the whole night in excruciating detail (the crab fondue, the tears, the histrionic way his mother had said she'd 'robbed him of grandchildren' and thrown herself across the settee).

In the end, Jake had called his uncle Martin, who had written a check and told Jake to use the money to get a white baby. 'You think you can handle another-race child,' said Martin, who had left his long-suffering white wife for Celeste, a young Hispanic waitress at Lone Wolf. 'But I'm helping you in the end, and that's the truth.'

Were we equipped to raise a nonwhite baby? One issue, obviously, would be bigoted relatives like Martin. (We'd opened a file with a local agency and checked the box confirming we wanted a healthy baby of any color.)

I believed in my heart I would be a great

165

mom, not perfect, but as good as I could possibly be. I worked hard and wanted to share my love, to be a part of something bigger than me. I remembered playing with my Raggedy Ann at age four, feeding her, swaddling her, holding her until she fell apart. I'd be a mother like my mom. Just there — quiet, kind, supportive. Like a warm bed beneath someone, a warm Barcalounger who smelled good. A Barcalounger who made snacks and brought them to your room, not interrupting your play date, just leaving buttered popcorn in a bowl by the door.

★   ★   ★

I shook my head to clear it. Lainey was waiting. 'Gosh, who knows?' I said. 'Holidays, you know?'

We did, in fact, visit Lockhart every year for the holidays, but pretty much avoided Jake's family otherwise. He had let them down by marrying me. What on earth was there to say?

25

Carla

The moon was the same, which seemed impossible. Although I was violated, broken — although the world as I had known it was gone — the blanket of light over our bodies as the train rushed forward was identical to the glow that had bathed me moments before, when I believed God was protecting me.

I arranged my clothing and sat up. No one said a word, as if we could will my rape away if we never spoke of it. We were afraid. The train moved fast and noisily. The hours, then days, dragged along. It was hot. We were thirsty. Every time the train slowed, bad people climbed aboard, and did what they wanted with us and to us. After a few days, we had little left — the men (and they were always men — or boys, some as young as Ernesto) took our water, our blankets, our clothes. We were treated as nothing, as bodies atop a train. I saw a child fall to his death. I saw a man's leg crushed when the train rolled over him. I saw things I don't want to repeat and don't want to think about.

By the time *la migra* caught me, it was a relief.

26

Alice

We drove to Jake's parents' house, a large brick colonial with Romanesque columns flanking the front door. Winifred, who had designed the house herself, said the style was 'neoeclectic.' We parked, and when Jake opened the door to let me and Pete out, I smelled smoke. It seemed Collin had been up early (or late) working in his own pit. 'Do you smell what I smell?' I said to Jake.

'Yup,' said Jake. 'Guess he's strutting his stuff.'

I smiled, kissed Jake on his stubbled cheek. 'What did you expect?' I said.

'I guess I'd hoped . . . ' said Jake.

'That you'd get the spotlight? Honey, please.'

'Right, I know you're right,' said Jake. Lainey hovered nearby, pretending not to eavesdrop. 'Off the record, obviously,' said Jake, and she nodded, murmuring apologies but not turning off her recorder.

Jake's parents were superstars. Of course, they weren't going to let a *Bon Appétit* magazine article pass them by. Winifred answered the door with a wide smile, ushering Lainey inside with a sweep of her plump arm, squinting to locate a photographer who was not in attendance. (They would send someone for photos later, we'd been told, after Lainey's story had been written and approved.) Winifred wore a red strapless dress and snakeskin boots, her hair piled high in a style I hadn't seen before. (I had, however, spotted her hairstylist, Betty, driving away from the house as we pulled in. Betty was brought in to style my hair on occasion, as Winifred wasn't a fan of my 'clumpy ponytail look,' as she called it.)

'Welcome,' said Winifred. '*Bon Appétit!* I declare! We subscribe.'

'That's great,' said Lainey. 'It's an honor to meet you.'

'Oh, pish,' said Winifred. 'Fried deviled egg? Bloody Mary?' Before we had answered, Lupita and her daughter Chandra appeared in their uniforms, bearing silver trays. 'Hope you don't mind,' said Winifred. 'We've invited a few close chums to brunch.'

Jake sighed, but Lainey seemed enthusiastic. She held out her recorder and followed Winifred into the dining room, which was filled with Lockhart celebrities and (it seemed) the entire Lockhart Lions football team in uniform. Lupita handed me a fried deviled egg and squeezed my hand. 'I'm sorry about the baby,' she said. Tears sprang to my eyes, and she pulled me into a floral-scented hug, then pushed a Bloody Mary into my free hand. Lupita had been with Jake's family since he was a child; Winifred had hired her during a Cancún vacation and had liked having a nanny so much, she'd arranged to bring sixteen-year-old Lupita back to Lockhart at the end of their trip. I'd never asked the details, but Lupita had moved into the Conroe manse, freeing Winifred up to plan events and play tennis. Jake loved Lupita like a mother. (In this case, maybe even *more* than a mother. Or equally, for certain.)

Lupita had left a boyfriend behind in Cancún, and when she told the Conroes she wanted to go back and marry him, they (somehow) brought Jesus to Texas as well. A talented farmer, Jesus was tasked with growing all the vegetables needed for Harrison's side dishes. Eventually he was hired by Lone Wolf, too, and after a long career, he had recently retired and taken up topiary gardening.

Lupita, Jesus, and their children lived next door to the Conroes in a miniature version of the columned brick home, and Jesus created whimsical hedges all over town. A Jesus

Melendez garden was much prized among Lockhart society, Winifred told Lainey, leading her past the dining table to the backyard, where Jake's father, Collin, was smoking meat alongside the Noah's Ark topiary. 'And he *just this week* added the baby pandas,' Winifred said into Lainey's recorder. 'Can you see them? Right next to the giraffes? It's hell to keep them watered in the summer, but you do what you have to do for *art*, know what I mean?'

'Stupendous,' proclaimed Lainey.

'You might *think* you've tasted the best brisket in the state of Texas, but you haven't tasted my goddamn brisket, so you're wrong!' boomed Collin, who I guessed had been practicing this exaltation all night.

'Oh, really?' said Lainey coquettishly.

'Goddamn right!' said Collin. 'Hi, honey,' he added, in a softer voice, holding out his arm to me. I settled in for a one-armed hug; Collin was tending the meat, and I knew better than to expect him to put down the metal spatula. He kissed the top of my head. 'You okay, girl?' he asked.

I nodded, lifting my chin.

He cupped his hand over the back of my hair. 'God's plan,' he said quietly. 'God's plan.'

I did not respond, but wriggled free and

went around to the side yard to have a minute to myself. I sat down next to what might have been zebras or maybe horses crafted from yew, and tried to breathe evenly. How the fuck, I wondered, was it God's plan for me to be infertile? For Mitchell's mom to give me one night of bliss before taking him away? As Jake had asked that night, drunk with sadness and tequila, what was the point of this pain? If you believed there was a plan, then what the fuck was the end game here?

I didn't believe there was a plan. Look at Evian, for Christ's sake. What was the plan for her? God had given her a shitty mother, then hooked her up with someone like me, who hadn't a clue about how to help her. What was I supposed to do? How could I change this situation? I felt angry and impotent.

But then I thought — why not? I wanted to take care of someone, and Evian sure as hell needed care. I took out my phone and called her, readying myself to do *something* — whatever was needed. Evian answered on the second ring. 'Alice?' she said.

'Hi,' I said. 'I'm just checking in. How are — '

'I'm fine,' she said coldly.

'Okay,' I said. 'Good, I'm glad to hear that.'

'Not that you care,' said Evian.

'What? Evian, you know I — '

'Not that you'd answer your phone when I need you.'

'Evian!' I said.

'Look, you don't need to call me anymore.'

'Please, Evian,' I said. 'Listen. Let's plan — '

But she had cut the line.

I slipped my phone back into my pocket. I sat inside the topiary for a while.

★　★　★

Lunch was elaborate and delicious. Winifred had invited not only the football team but a chef visiting from Paris named Daniel, who gave Lainey a great quote as he hoisted his pork rib. 'Meat with handles,' he declared in his sultry accent, 'it is always a good thing.'

'Hear, hear!' said Collin, raising his Shiner.

★　★　★

After lunch, the guests departed, and Lainey perched on the cowhide sofa to interview Jake with his parents. I wandered upstairs, curling into Jake's childhood bed. It was unchanged from when he was in high school, the flannel sheets smelling faintly of Polo cologne. I couldn't get comfortable in my tight-waisted

174

dress, so I climbed from the bed to rummage in the bureau for a T-shirt. I slid open the top drawer, but instead of Jake's old stuff, I saw a pale blue blanket. I took it from the drawer with a sickening feeling. It was new and impossibly soft.

I spread the small blanket across the bed and touched the white embroidery at the edge — elegant script, spelling 'Mitchell.'

★ ★ ★

I don't know how long I'd been staring at the name when Winifred pushed open the door. 'Oh, honey,' she exhaled.

'Hi,' I said.

Winifred sat down next to me on her son's bed. She wasn't looking at me but out the window, which faced the football stadium. I thought about how awful it must have been for Jake to sit in this room, his knee blown, listening to the crowds across the street cheering for a team he wasn't on. 'I'm sorry you found the blanket,' said Winifred. 'I didn't want to . . . throw it away.'

'I understand,' I said.

'Well, here's some news: we're selling Martin the restaurant,' said Winifred. 'We don't have any more money to lose.'

'Oh,' I said.

'Don't know if he'll change the name,' said Winifred. 'I don't care, to be honest. The Lone Wolf! What a jackass.' She sighed. 'Collin can damn well cook for *me* every night,' she said.

'Maybe not brisket . . . maybe Italian,' I said. She turned to me, amused, then laughed.

'Maybe *Indian*,' she said. We both began to giggle, sharing a joke few women would understand. Winifred shook her head and leaned against the wall, crossing her boots. She seemed frail, and I realized how much energy this party must have cost her. She was deflated without an audience. 'There's some good news, too,' she said. She took an envelope from her pocket and handed it to me. 'It's money,' she said. 'Do with it what you will.'

'Oh,' I said. 'Thank you, Winifred.'

'How much for the Mormon baby?'

'The what?'

'Didn't you tell me about a cheap private adoption? Some Utah organization?'

'Oh, right,' I said, nodding. 'Thirty thousand.'

She frowned. 'Here I thought ten would solve all your problems. Thirty, well, that's a different animal altogether.'

I smiled. 'I appreciate it, Winifred, really.' I held the envelope toward her, but my fingers wouldn't let go. I tried to be calm, but my mind was whirring — maybe we could try international again? There had to be some country somewhere that would let a forty-one-year-old adopt. Or we could find another surrogate? Maybe if we bought a bigger house and updated our file with a more impressive address? Maybe, somehow, something . . .

'It's yours,' said Winifred. 'I'm sorry it's not enough.'

'Me too,' I said. 'I'm sorry *I'm* not enough,' I added, surprising myself.

Winifred turned. 'What is *that* supposed to mean?' she said, arching a perfectly plucked eyebrow.

'Nothing,' I said. 'Forget it.'

But instead of standing up and leaving — which was her specialty — Winifred stayed next to me. 'You are every mother's dream,' she said. I snorted. 'Don't you think I see how much he loves you?' said Winifred. 'Don't you know how proud we are of what you two have made? Of course we wish we had grandbabies — I'd take a hundred, from anyplace on earth. Martin's a damn fool with his *white baby* bullshit — can you see why I married his brother?'

I was crying, but nodded.

'I wish you had children, honey,' said Winifred. 'But what you have already

. . . that's all I could ever hope for, for *my* baby — a love like yours. Don't you know how lucky you are?'

And then, in her patented Winifred Conroe maneuver, she stood up and exited, leaving me in tears.

★ ★ ★

On our way back to Austin, we drove through downtown, stopping to let Lainey wander the hallways and pits of Harrison's BBQ. She exclaimed over the famous sign at the doorway:

NO BARBECUE SAUCE
(Nothing to Hide)

NO FORKS
(They Are at the End of Your Arm)

NO CREDIT CARDS
(The Bank Doesn't Take Barbecue)

NO KIDDING
(See Owner's Face)

She took multiple snapshots, then wandered around, speaking softly into her phone, trying to describe the place. Though I had once thought of being a writer, watching Lainey — the way she had to slip outside of every experience to figure out how to explain it to others — made me glad I'd ended up behind the Conroe's counter. If I tried to convey the way Harrison's rooms smelled (smoky, salty, permanent, enveloping) or, for that matter, the way Jake's brisket made me feel (cared for, satiated, warm, grateful), the words I came up with fell short so monumentally that it felt like shooting a bird to appreciate its feathers.

In the end, all the fetishism around Jake's brisket was interesting, and I knew it made him proud, the way people wanted to know about his process. He worked hard, after all, alone in the night watching fire. But I thought all the details — what wood, what temperature, the chemical composition of collagen — took away from the experience of picking up Jake's meat between your thumb and forefinger, placing it into your mouth, closing your eyes, and letting a wave — an indescribable wave — wash over you. It was delicious, sure, and you could ponder the bark all day, but that was beside the point.

From behind the counter, I got to watch the faces: Officer Grupo after a long night, a student unmoored in the world, a grandmother nobody cooked for anymore. They chewed, and felt cared for. Their faces were children's — all pretense sliding away, revealing the most essential needs met. *Mom's on time to pick me up after choir. Dad's scratching my back even after he thinks I've fallen asleep. I love you, from someone you dare love. I am hungry, and being fed.*

★　★　★

That night, after we'd dropped Lainey at the Hotel Saint Cecilia, we returned home to Mildred Street. As Jake watched baseball, Pete next to him on the couch, I went into the small garden we had planted in the back. Not much came up in summer, so I had hit the farmer's market that morning. I went into our kitchen with a handful of arugula, turned the radio to a jazz station, and took off my boots. I cut the stalks off beets, placed them in a roasting pan, and slid it into the oven. I sliced squash, zucchini, and crisp asparagus spears, then sautéed the vegetables in my mother's cast-iron pan (it held the seasoning of a hundred campouts) with olive oil, salt, and pepper. I divided the buttery, bitter greens from our garden into two wide bowls, added the vegetables from Mom's pan, then broke a bit of queso fresco on top. When the beets were ready, I sliced them, the blood-red juice staining my fingers, and arranged them on the salads, adding more cheese, salt, and pepper. I poured two glasses of chilled white Burgundy.

And then, filled with a quiet sense of accomplishment and joy, I brought my husband his supper.

27

Carla

The Beast had stopped in a fair-sized town. Junior and I were sitting in the shade of a tin roof eating mangoes Ernesto had given us. He seemed to have acquaintances in every place; when the train slowed, he would step off, disappear for a while, and return with water and food. I had thought he was running from his gang, but he no longer seemed scared. We never talked about what had happened to me.

In the town where I was caught by *la migra*, Ernesto was smoking cigarettes with a group of boys who had the number on their faces. We were waiting for the train to begin moving again, so we could jump aboard.

'I'll be right back,' said my brother, standing up and stepping into the sunlight.

'Where are you going?' I asked. I had a guess; he found a way to refill his baby-food jar at most rest stops. I didn't know if people gave him the glue or if he stole it. I hoped that our mother could help my brother get well in Austin, Texas.

Junior ambled off, toward Ernesto and his gang of thugs. I took a juicy bite of mango flesh into my mouth, the taste giving me pleasure. All of a sudden, a truck approached with sirens blaring and someone shouted, '¡La migra! ¡La policia!'

'Junior!' I hollered, jumping to my feet. I began to sprint toward my brother, but Junior was also running, following Ernesto away from the town square, toward the ramshackle houses that lay beyond it.

He did not turn. My brother, whom I spent every night curled around, my nose nestled in his earthy-smelling hair. He never glanced toward me, just pumped his legs forward, his arms moving rhythmically as he fled. I tried to catch up.

An immigration officer caught me by the wrist. I howled, tried to wrench free, but it felt like an alligator had clamped its teeth on my arm. 'Ernesto!' I screamed.

Ernesto slowed. He looked back: his lovely face with its terrible black tattoo, his mouth open, gasping for air.

'Take care of my brother!' I cried.

Did I imagine it? Perhaps. But it seemed that Ernesto nodded — a promise — then turned again and ran.

'Come with me, miss,' said the officer. Three other officials were grabbing people;

they handcuffed us and shoved us into air-conditioned trucks. If anyone protested, they were beaten. I did not protest. A part of me was broken, tired, ready to just go home. I did not understand what God wanted from me, and where He was taking me, and why.

We were piled on top of each other, taken to a squat cement building, a jail, where one by one we were interviewed. I knew what I was supposed to do in this instance: pretend I was Mexican, so as not to be sent back home. My brother was in Mexico now, in the company of a boy I did not understand or trust. It was my duty to find Junior.

So when the woman asked me the name of the president of Honduras, I told her I had no idea. When she asked who the Mexican president was, I said proudly, 'Vicente Fox.'

The woman shook her head. 'Vicente Fox was the president of Mexico many years ago,' she said. 'Look. I can put you on that bus, and you will be in Tegucigalpa tomorrow morning.'

Just hearing the name of my city melted my insides. I thought of Humberto, his lips, his curling black hair. I thought of my house, the pallet where I could sleep unmolested. But then I thought of Junior, so small, adrift in Chiapas.

'I am Mexican,' I said. 'I just forgot! Of

course, the new president is . . . ' She waited, but no name came to me. More specifically, only *one* name came to me: Vicente Fox. 'The new president is . . . ' I said, helplessly.

The woman watched me with patience. Her eyes were so soft I wished for a moment that she would adopt me herself. I had to force myself to stay in my plastic chair instead of leaping into her lap and begging her to save me.

'The president of Mexico is . . . ,' I repeated. I held my breath and bit my lip, praying for the answer to appear in my mind. I put one tired foot on top of the other. I wrapped my arms around myself, digging my fingernails into my skin. I stared at the official, wondered if she had children, if she sang lullabies at night.

'Yes?' said the woman. She held her pen aloft, ready to seal my fate. Outside the jail, a row of buses idled, waiting to return us to the places we belonged.

28

Alice

After dinner, we got into bed. Lazily, Jake kissed my neck, then my collarbones, my breasts. I turned to him. We made love tenderly at first, and then frantically, as if trying to reach a place we'd lost the directions to. Was he thinking about Lainey? I was thinking of myself, in a way — how I might look from above, my hair tangled, nightgown abandoned, moving above my husband, his eyes closed, large hands grasping at the meat of my waist. We both climaxed, technically, but I felt far away from Jake, and for that matter, far away from myself. This was a strange time in our marriage: we were being fashioned into personalities by reporters like Lainey, but we were losing sight of who we'd hoped to be, who we were, and what the hell we wanted.

★   ★   ★

Jake was leaving town in the morning, so he rose around 10:00 p.m. to head into Conroe's and prepare the ribs for the next day. I was still wide awake and decided to join him. Through rainy streets, we drove to the restaurant, detouring to grab pastries from La Mexicana Bakery. The fecund scent of Austin — the smell of things growing; too many things, growing too fast, but thrillingly so — calmed me, brought me back to myself. Why had making love with Jake left me unmoored? I decided not to think about it.

At Conroe's, we worked together soundlessly, classical music on the radio. Pete slept in his crate. Around midnight, I was cutting fat from a brisket when I heard a rapping on the window. I looked up and saw Evian standing in the rain outside Conroe's.

'Honey?' said Jake.

'It's my deal,' I said.

'Damn right it is,' said Jake.

I washed my hands and pushed open the door. Evian saw me and rushed forward. 'Oh, Alice!' she cried, throwing herself against me, a wet storm of fruity-smelling body spray and booze. There was a dull thud as the side of her face hit my rib cage. I hesitated for a moment, stunned, but then slowly lifted my arms and folded them around her skinny shoulders. 'My mom kicked me out,' said Evian, her voice rapid-fire and muffled against my shirt. 'She hates Sam. She won't let me smoke. I can't handle it! I can't handle it!' Evian sobbed wildly for a while. I patted her shiny jacket.

Over her head, I watched the kitchen nervously, afraid that Jake would see our embrace and be angry. I could see the little painted sign I'd hung above the refrigerator: *Home is where the heart is*. I'd found it in the pile of trash the previous owners had left in the living room of our Mildred Street house. I'd also found some beat-up pots and pans and a Crock-Pot that worked fine once you duct-taped the crack in the lid. I found it surprisingly easy to feel hopeful when I read the plaque, rather than focusing on the fact that the previous owners of our house had perhaps given up on the sentiment while packing for Pflugerville.

'Shh, shh. What can I do?' I said.

She took a deep breath and pulled back, presenting me with her tear-stained face, made grotesque by some sort of multicolored mascara. It's not that I fell for her histrionics, but I remembered clearly being a teenager and wanting a mother. I guess I saw a bit of myself in Evian, though we hadn't had the sort of face paint Evian favored at the Ouray Variety Store. Her pupils were wide, and I tried to remember if this meant she was drunk or stoned.

'I don't have anywhere to go!' she cried. 'Sam doesn't have a house! He lives with the football coach. I can't go there!'

'Sam lives with the football coach?' I asked.

'He's the *quarterback*!' Evian wailed. This was surprising news, as Sam was certainly tall but not very broad. Maybe he was the JV quarterback. Sometimes it seemed as if every man I met in Texas was, wanted to be, or had been a quarterback.

'His mother's on drugs,' cried Evian. 'I have nowhere to go!'

'I'll take you home,' I said. 'Let me get my keys.'

'No!' shrieked Evian, folding inward and howling as if someone had kicked her in the spleen. Jake came to the door.

'Alice?' he called, pushing open the screen.

'Here,' I said. 'I'm here, with Evian.'

'Oh. I see,' said Jake. He went back inside, not stopping the screen door from slamming (as he knew it would) with an emphatic *bam*. He couldn't have planned it better: *Oh. I see. Bam!*

'Wait here,' I told Evian.

★ ★ ★

In the kitchen, Jake was making coffee-chipotle sauce. He raised his eyebrows when I

189

came in. 'Her mother kicked her out,' I said.

'I'm sorry to hear that,' said Jake evenly. He looked old under the fluorescent lights. I saw fine lines around his eyes that I'd never noticed before.

We both leaned against the steel counters we'd salvaged from a restaurant on South Lamar when the owner had been arrested for trafficking heroin. 'I think I'm going to tell her she can stay with us tonight, and that's all,' I ventured.

Jake whisked with fervor. He set the metal bowl down sharply, snapped his head up, and said, 'I disagree.'

'Noted,' I said, pushing the door open and stepping outside.

'This is a really important week for me,' said Jake. 'Lainey's here for six more days.'

'Fuck off,' I told him.

I went to Evian and took her hand. 'You can sleep on our couch,' I told her, leading her to the truck.

'Thank you,' she said. I noticed she was dragging a large garbage bag, which she explained was her belongings. ('Mostly dirty laundry,' she told me.) I couldn't tell if I had done the right thing, but I felt strong at least, as if I was taking charge of something.

I made Evian a bed on the couch with a sleeping bag and two pillows. I even found a mini-tube of Crest and an extra toothbrush that had probably not been used before. I brought her a washcloth and a bar of soap and told her to sleep tight. Pete had stayed at Conroe's with Jake.

'Hey, Alice?' called Evian as I was changing into pajamas.

'Yes?'

'Do you have, like, a Wi-Fi password?'

'Oh, sure,' I said. I jotted it down, *WHERESTHEBEEF*, and brought it to Evian, who seemed to have recovered completely from her previous hysteria. She sat on the couch in my pajamas with her legs crossed, tapping away at her device. I went into my room and tried to fall asleep, but sleep would not come. After a while, I heard the front door open. Jake tiptoed to our room, changed quickly, and climbed into bed.

'I'm awake,' I whispered.

'I have to get some rest,' said Jake. 'Lainey and I are leaving in a few hours.' Since Jake had told Lainey about the different styles of Texas barbecue — hickory-smoked and slathered with sauce in East Texas; South Texas *barbacoa*, beef heads smoked in a hole in the ground; direct-heat, mesquite-flavored 'cowboy style' in West Texas — she'd gotten the go-ahead from her editor to take Jake on the road. 'Are you sure you and Benji can handle the rush?' asked Jake.

'We'll be fine,' I said.

'She can't live here,' said Jake.

I breathed out. 'She has nowhere else to go,' I said.

Jake spoke with a measured calm, as if he had practiced his words on the walk home. 'I know you wanted a baby,' he said. 'I know how much you want to . . . take care of someone. But this girl isn't ours. She needs more help than we can give.'

'Noted,' I said.

Jake paused. I knew he was fighting the urge to yell. 'When I get home from the trip, I don't want her here,' said Jake, his voice tight. 'Is that *noted*?'

'I can't promise anything,' I said. 'I'm sorry.'

'I'm saying this with love, but I don't really like who you're turning into,' said Jake.

I turned from him, curled into myself.

Jake spoke quietly, his voice deadly sad. 'I know you're disappointed with our life,' he said.

I was quiet. He was right.

'I've worked so hard — we both have, Al . . . and you are always . . . you are *still* disappointed. I hate myself for that. But you know what, Al? I want to be happy. If you can't even try to be proud, or even the tiniest bit satisfied, I don't know what to say. I can only disappoint you for so long. It's killing me.'

'Jake . . . ' I said.

'Yes?'

The hope that I would say the right thing — that I was satisfied; that I didn't want a child, not anymore; that I would stop fighting God's plan, would stop trying to fashion a baby out of a dog or an opportunistic teenager named after a brand of bottled water — hung in the air, it must be said, like smoke. And then it dissipated. Jake rolled over and closed his eyes.

★ ★ ★

I must have fallen asleep, because something woke me — the sound of a car pulling up to our house. The clock radio on my nightstand read 4:03. Stumbling from bed, I went into the living room to see that the couch was empty. I heard voices outside, and pushed open the front door.

'Evian?' I called. 'What are you doing?'

Two men sat on my porch swing. One wore a leather jacket and one a sleeveless T-shirt. Both were smoking, dropping ash onto the ground. 'She's having a little discussion,' said the one in the jacket. He watched me steadily, and I felt scared. They were drinking something brown from crystal glasses that had been my mom's.

'Don't worry, Ms. Conroe,' said Evian. She was leaning against a post, and had dressed and reapplied her makeup. She also held one of my mother's glasses.

'Evian, come back inside,' I said.

She laughed, and the men laughed with her. 'Let's roll,' said the one in the jacket, and the two men stood. The swing crashed into the side of our house. Evian tossed my mother's glass onto the lawn and followed the men down the steps and toward a sedan with tinted windows.

'Evian!' I cried. 'Come back here!'

I ran down the walk and grabbed her arm before she could get in the car. She yanked it back with force. 'Who do you think you are?' she hissed. 'You're giving me a couch to sleep on, lady, you're not my mother!'

She slid into the passenger seat and slammed the door, and the car peeled away. I stood by the street, my hand covering my mouth. Who *did* I think I was? Who?

29

Carla

I lay awake on a mattress as thick as my wrist. When I moved my body, the springs complained. The smell of urine filled my nose. In my whole life, I had never slept by myself, and I couldn't stop thinking of my brother, whom I had failed. I prayed for assistance, though I was no longer sure that anyone was listening.

By the time my interview had concluded, the last bus of the day was gone. I supposed I would be transported back to Honduras in the morning. I am ashamed to remember how close I came to losing faith during my night in the Mexican jail.

I finally fell into a deep sleep, and I saw Humberto. He was waiting for me inside my grandmother's house. Without Junior, Humberto and I could make a life together. I had not sold my crumbling home; I had left in haste and without the thought that I would return. But in my dream, Humberto had swept the floor and filled the kitchen with ingredients. I could even smell onions frying.

Humberto opened his arms and held me — not in a romantic way, but as if I were a baby needing comfort.

After what had happened to my body, I no longer wanted to kiss Humberto, or anyone. All I wanted was a motherly embrace. I wanted my mother. I hurt.

In the dream, Humberto fed me with a warm wooden spoon. There were bad people outside the house, but Humberto had installed a large padlock. I felt a fragile peace.

When a guard opened the cell door in the morning, I jumped up, all the calm of my dream falling from me as if it were a skin I had outgrown. The guard's eyes slid up and down my body like hungry hands. I looked at the floor and prayed he would not touch me. 'You have family in America?' he said. His voice was rough, and my heart beat terribly, thumping at my rib cage as if it would escape.

'My mother,' I whispered. I must have been somewhat delirious. 'I want my mother,' I said. My eyes filled stupidly with tears.

'Breakfast,' he said, handing me a tray of bread and water and then closing the cell again. I dried my eyes and ate.

The bus to Honduras was empty but for me and one man, a skinny man with thick eyebrows. It made me upset to think about the cost of the gasoline to drive me and one man all the way back to Tegu. I could have fed Junior for a year with the money. I tried not to ask God why He would allow this, but a voice in my head said anyway, 'Why?' Maybe God was taking care of the man who owned the bus, or the old man who drove us, his expression placid as a cow's.

The bus lumbered to the edge of town. I rested my head on the seat, looking out the dusty window. It was early in the day, most of the shops still shuttered, no children playing outside. The driver turned down an alley. Sharply, the bus pulled to the side and stopped. I sat up, panic igniting in my veins. The other Honduran looked relaxed, as if he knew what was going on. My mouth was dry; I waited. The voice I could not silence in my mind said, *Please, God. Please, God.* The driver opened the door.

The Honduran man with the large eyebrows stood. 'It's your lucky day, little girl,' he said. 'Come.' I lifted my gaze, unsure if I had heard him correctly.

'Let's go,' he repeated.

My mouth opened. I was scared, wondering what he wanted from me. (I figured it was going to hurt, whatever it was.) I rose and stepped hesitantly toward the man, expecting him to grab me, force me down.

We moved toward the door of the bus and

the driver did not look at us, just waited. We stepped into the alleyway. The Honduran man bid me to follow him, and I did, ducking behind a building. The bus started up and drove away.

'You can go,' said the man, once we were out of sight. 'Unless you have money for the *coyote*. What an idiot! But at least he paid the Zetas in time.' He rubbed his eyes.

I didn't know what he was talking about, though I understand now. The drug cartels in Mexico run everything from the prisons to the human-smuggling *coyotes*. If a *coyote* falls behind on payments, his cargo is taken away. As soon as my fellow passenger's *coyote* paid the Zetas (who controlled the town we were in), the cartel ordered his release. God had not left me alone. He had put me on a bus that would not leave town.

I took advantage of God's kindness, the first good thing anyone had done for me in some time. I looked up and down the street, then began to run. I pushed my sore legs against the ground, breathing deeply, moving fast. In the distance, I heard the siren of the train. I could climb atop the train at any time, I knew. I could find my brother, and bring him to America. God was with me.

30

Alice

I woke to the smell of coffee. Bleary-eyed, I pulled on my ratty robe and opened the bedroom door. Jake was frying eggs in the kitchen next to Lainey, who wore a leather miniskirt and boots that came up above her knees. Her hair was in a bun on the very top of her head, a look I didn't understand but surmised was chic. Lainey leaned close, smelling Jake's pan. I put my shoulders back and ran my fingers through my hair, wishing desperately that I had a more glamorous robe to pull on . . . a kimono, something silk. 'Oh, hey,' said Lainey. 'I'm so sorry, did we wake you?'

'Not at all,' I said breezily. I made my way quickly to the bathroom, but the door was locked.

'Evian's in the shower,' said Jake without inflection.

'It's *so funny* you have a teenager on your couch,' said Lainey. 'Named Evian,' she added.

'Oh, she just needed a place to crash, you know?' I said, my words coming fast and screechy, as if I had no control over my mouth.

'This house is *adorable*,' said Lainey. 'It is *so cute*. In New York, this place would be huge!'

I went back inside the bedroom and closed the door. There was nothing for me to add to the breakfast confab. I sat down on the bed, considering climbing back under the covers. Instead, I opened my bureau drawer and found a sweater dress that was a bit pilled and stretched out. I took off my pajamas, donned the dress, and added turquoise vintage boots and lipstick. I brushed my hair and pulled it back. Thinking of Evian, I applied mascara. I threw open the bedroom door for the second time, feeling more ready to defend my house and husband. 'I love eggs!' I trilled.

Lainey was already out the door, trailed by Pete, who leapt into the truck. Jake had his overnight duffel in his hand. 'Oh,' he said, 'I'm sorry, there wasn't enough ... ' I followed his gaze to the kitchen, where two plates and the frying pan sat in a sink full of soapy water. 'There's some coffee,' said Jake.

'Okay,' I said.

'We've got to get going,' said Jake.

'Sure,' I said.

Jake smiled at me, and I smiled back. 'I love those boots,' he said.

'And I love your — ' My sexy statement

was cut short by the bathroom door slamming open and Evian appearing in a cloud of fruit-scented steam, a toothbrush in one hand, her phone in the other. She wore tight jeans and a midriff-baring T-shirt.

'Adios,' said Jake, exiting quickly and jogging toward Lainey, who could be heard saying, 'I love your neighborhood's *atmosphere*. Like East Village meets Rio meets . . . Perth!'

'You're out of shampoo,' said Evian, sitting on the couch, staring at her phone.

'Evian,' I said. 'We need to talk about what happened last night.'

Obsequiously, she folded her hands in her lap and looked up. 'Yes?' she said.

'Who were those men?'

'I'm going to be late for school, Ms. Conroe,' she said. 'Maybe we can talk about this later? Um, are you driving me?'

'I guess so,' I said, filling my mug with coffee.

As we made our way to the car, Evian commented, 'If I were you, Ms. Conroe, I'd keep my eye on that New York slut with the meth bun.'

'Evian!' I said, unlocking the car doors. 'You can't use language like that, honey. Honestly. If you want people to take you seriously, you need to be more careful about how you present yourself.'

'But am I right, Ms. Conroe?'

I started the car and sighed. 'You may be,' I acceded.

We drove toward Chávez. I knew I should force her to explain the previous night's antics and then tell her she couldn't stay with me anymore, but I was worn out. 'You can drop me here,' said Evian a few blocks from school.

'I'll take you to the front door,' I said.

'Yeah,' she said, 'if we don't show up they're gonna close us.'

'Hmm?' I asked.

'They're trying to close our school,' said Evian. '*Again*. Don't you read the papers? We're not worth it. If they close Chávez, I'm dropping out. I am *not* going back to Travis.'

'They won't close the school,' I said.

'Attendance is an issue,' said Evian. 'Also, the testing is an issue. We're too dumb.' She laughed hollowly. 'And too many pregnant.'

I pulled into the parking lot and saw Marion Markson cheerily playing crossing guard. She hugged some students as they approached, stopped others to speak to them seriously, meeting their eyes. She wore a bright orange pantsuit and seemed to laugh easily. 'Oh, Lord, Principal Markson's waiting out front,' said Evian, smiling and shaking her head. 'Tell you what, Ms. Conroe,' she added, raising her eyebrows. 'They close Chávez, the one I'm most worried about is Principal Markson. That lady is *really* into this school.'

'She is the principal,' I said primly.

'Yeah, we're lucky,' said Evian. She leaned over and hugged me quickly. 'See you tonight!' she said, alighting from the car and jogging toward school. I spotted Sam in a crisp letter jacket, standing by the door. When Evian reached him, he grinned and put his arm around her shoulder. She turned back and waved to me, then approached Principal Markson, who greeted the couple warmly and shooed them inside. As I drove out of the parking lot, I saw Officer Grupo, leaning against his squad car and sipping a Big Gulp soda. I raised my hand as I drove past and he gave me a thumbs-up.

Chávez looked different in the early morning. It seemed hopeful, a happy place, a refuge. I was glad to be a part of it.

★ ★ ★

That afternoon, Principal Markson came in for a Sweet Stacy. I handed her the sandwich, and she eyed the plate hungrily. The line behind her was long, but I said, 'Principal Markson?'

'Marion, please!' she said.

'I wanted to talk to you . . . about Evian.'

'Oh,' she said, surprised. 'I'm not sure if this is the best place.'

'She's staying with me,' I said. 'I don't know if . . . '

Marion's phone buzzed, and she held up her hand. 'Let's talk another time,' she said. 'Are you free Friday night?'

'Uh,' I said. 'Yes, actually. Sure. Coffee?'

'Hold on, please,' said Marion into her phone. To me, she said, 'I could use a real drink, if you want to know the truth. You know Donn's Depot on Fifth?'

'Yeah,' I said. It was a dim cantina with a cocktail waitress who could remember your name even if you hadn't been in for years. For some reason, the entire place was decorated with Christmas lights year-round.

'Friday night at eight?'

'Sounds great,' I said. And it did sound great. I needed some counsel and I needed a ladies' night out. I served the man after Marion with a smile.

★ ★ ★

After Benji and I had cleaned up and closed Conroe's for the day, I went home and picked up Evian's things and our dirty clothes, heading to Frank's Coin Laundry. I'd found a copy of *Mr. Bridge* at a used-book store, and I read it while the washer ran. It was sad to read about someone so fully devoted to his work that he didn't see his wife, though she was right next to him. I knew there was a companion novel, *Mrs. Bridge*, about how her life had played out alongside his. After transferring the clothes to the dryer, I thought about my mom and dad. Their lives had been impossibly, perfectly entwined. I had always thought this was what I wanted, but when my mom had died, my father was no longer whole.

I brought the laundry home and folded Evian's things, her tiny underwear and T-shirts, her jeans and miniskirts. I went into Mitchell's nursery and dismantled the crib, emptied the bureau of baby clothes, gathered the diapers and baby toys from the closet, and put it all in the storage shed in the backyard. In the crib's place, I put an inflated camping mattress with clean sheets and pillows. I stacked Evian's things in the bureau, gazing only for a moment at the baby bunny I had painted on its side.

31

Carla

I had been jailed in the same town where I had lost my brother. He and Ernesto might have climbed a train in the hours I was asleep, but I went searching for them anyway. By the time I reached the plaza in which I had been apprehended, the sun was so white that everything appeared to be covered in a film of sand. The metal tracks were empty, glinting. I hated The Beast, and yet I needed The Beast to reach my mother.

I knew I could not remain in the station. Stumbling down a narrow street, I saw a dark doorway and a sign that said 'El Bambi.' I had watched the movie *Bambi* in the window of the PriceSmart electronics store. I am not stupid, but I was lost and tired, and a brothel seemed as good as any place to go.

Inside El Bambi, there was little light. The floor and the bar were made of concrete, and a dozen white plastic tables were unoccupied. There was a smell of beer, sweat, and fried beef. A jukebox glowed, illuminating a fat woman in a gold dress. She turned toward me and narrowed her eyes. 'You shouldn't be here, little girl,' said the woman, who was maybe twenty years old. I could tell she was Honduran, with light skin and hair dyed red and pulled away from her face. The straps of her shoes cut into her feet. I knew about places like this: we had them in Tegu, and some of the girls I'd gone to school with worked inside. You danced in provocative clothing for men who bought you beer or gave you *fichas*, little plastic chips you could trade for money at the end of the night. Usually, you had sex with men for money, too, but some girls claimed they remained virgins. A girl named Patrice told me she could drink thirty beers in one night and still stand up, which was both impressive and very sad. I had tasted a beer once, and never again. It made my mouth feel as if I had ingested a cleaning product: numb and scalded simultaneously.

'I'm sorry,' I said to the *fichera*.

'Go on, go away,' she said, waving me off and turning her attention to the jukebox. She pressed some buttons and the Golden Rooster began to sing, his smooth voice making even his most violent lyrics sound divine. He had been famous in Honduras even before he was gunned down. The woman swayed her hips a bit. 'I loved him,' she said wistfully.

'I also loved him,' I said.

She turned to me, breathing out. She wore makeup all over her face and eyes and lips. 'You don't want to be here, I assure you,' she said. 'You're from Tegu?'

I nodded, flushing that my face gave me away. 'I'm trying to get to my mother. In Texas. I lost my brother yesterday.'

'Zetas?'

'No, he's not dead. He ran away from *la migra* by the train station.'

The woman wobbled, and it occurred to me that she might be on drugs or maybe Resistol. Finally she said mournfully, 'I have no one on the other side.'

Despite my circumstances, I felt blessed at this moment, thinking about my mother safe in Austin, Texas. Yearning rose in my throat.

'I know what I'm doing,' the woman said. 'I send money to my children, you know. They have a better life because of me.'

'Yes,' I said. I thought of my dresses, my shoes from Old Navy. For a moment I felt confused. But my mother worked at a restaurant that served chicken, I told myself. 'Do you serve chicken here?' I asked, my voice low and frightened.

'Are you hungry?' said the woman. I nodded. She went around the corner and called for food. Another *fichera* emerged, carrying a plate with chopped beef and a bowl full of soup. I rushed toward her, my mouth filling with saliva, my worries about my mother momentarily forgotten.

'Okay, little girl,' the second woman said, laughing. 'Sit down, sit down!' She was younger than the woman in the gold dress and wore very short shorts and a T-shirt that was very tight and ended before her stomach began. She placed the food on a table and handed me utensils that seemed clean enough.

Before I ate, I gathered my courage and said, 'I do not want to be a prostitute.' I hoped I was not rude, but wanted to be clear. The young *fichera* laughed, her earrings jangling. 'Nobody wants to be a prostitute,' she said. 'Go ahead, girl, eat.'

The food was hot and filling. I ate more quickly than was polite. When I emptied the soup bowl, the *ficheras* refilled it. 'Thank you,' I said when I was done. 'Thank you so much. God will bless you both.'

The woman in the gold said, 'Now listen. You can waitress here, and there's no need to do anything you don't want to do. We're happy.' She said the last with a steely glint in her eyes. She patted my hand forcefully.

'I need to find my brother,' I said.

'Ah, let her go,' said the woman who had

given me food. 'Horace isn't here yet, he'll never know.'

The older woman frowned, but did not object.

'I will take you to a shelter for migrants,' said the younger woman. 'It's run by a priest. It's for people like you.'

'Thank you,' I managed, tears of relief making my voice watery. 'Thank you very much.'

'Enough,' said the young *fichera*. 'I'll return soon,' she told the woman in gold, but that woman was already back at the jukebox, her eyes dreamy.

Outside, the sunlight was blinding. We took a right turn, then a left. After a while, we reached a high fence lined with barbwire. 'The priest who runs this shelter has been threatened many times,' said the woman. She put her hands on her hips. 'I wish you luck,' she said, and added, 'You know, your body is a credit card no matter what choices you make.'

'I don't understand,' I said, but I thought of the men who had attacked me, how the pain had earned me a place on the top of the train, how I was still alive.

'Ah, little girl, you will,' said the woman. She looked at me for a moment, touched my cheek. Then she turned and walked back toward La Bambi.

* * *

The building was painted white, the bars on the windows a tomato red. A large mural of Jesus welcomed me. In front of the shelter, a group of men and boys listened to a soccer game on the radio. They looked freshly washed, their hair wet, and I closed my eyes and prayed that this place was safe. A few dogs lay at their feet.

I glanced at the clothing line strung along the side of the building. A dozen shirts and pairs of pants hung limp in the morning sun. And then I saw it, a beacon, a promise of joy: Junior's blue shirt, held tightly by wooden clothespins.

32

Alice

By four that afternoon, I began to fret about Evian. I texted her, asking if she needed to be picked up at school, and she responded: *I'm fine*. I made spaghetti and meatballs for dinner, but by seven, she had not returned. I ate alone in front of the television, watching a Canadian couple search for an apartment in Beijing. One apartment had pool access, but the bathroom was very small. The next, in a gated community near the husband's new job, had a huge kitchen and room for parties, but it was kind of isolated and had a garden neither husband nor wife wanted to maintain. The wife was not the gardening type, she said, smiling nervously. The husband nodded wryly at her admission. He was the business type, it was clear, but what type *was* the wife? What was she going to do all day in Beijing? The couple had just had a 'dream wedding' in Toronto.

I refilled my plate during the commercial break.

The last apartment was located near

restaurants and coffee shops. It was small, with a weird contraption that looked like a metal drawer but was used to 'make dried vegetables and fruits.' The couple appeared unimpressed. The wife noted that she didn't really cook, and again the husband nodded by her side. 'I really like the balcony!' the woman yelled as she took in the busy streets below the third apartment. The husband said it was pretty loud.

I was worried for the couple from Canada. None of these apartments would work, it was clear. The problem was not Beijing. I thought about Mr. and Mrs. Bridge. I thought about me and Jake.

* * *

The phone rang during the next commercial break. It was Jake, back in Austin, calling from Conroe's. 'Hey!' I answered, my voice false and wrong.

'How did everything go today?' he asked.

'Fine,' I said. 'I'm just sitting here eating spaghetti. Want to join me?'

'Lainey wants to watch prep,' said Jake. 'She wants to follow the whole process.'

'Oh,' I said, imagining Lainey in a lawn chair next to Jake, how romantic the flickering light would be on her smooth visage. 'That sounds really fun,' I said. 'I can come, too.'

'Are you insane?' said Jake.

'Slightly,' I said.

'Is she gone?' said Jake.

'Who's that?' I said.

'Evian,' said Jake.

'Oh, Evian!' I said. The television was muted, but I could see that the Canadian couple had chosen the gated community. On the screen, the wife appeared with a watering can and trowel, smiling unhappily in her huge new garden. 'She's not here now,' I said cagily.

There was silence on the line. 'I need you to take her home,' said Jake finally. 'We need some time to find ourselves again. Okay? We've been through a lot, honey. I'm asking you for this, and it's important to me. I just want to come home to my wife. Please.'

I didn't say anything, remembering how good it had felt to put clean clothes in the drawers of the bunny bureau. 'Hello?' said Jake. 'Do you hear me?'

'I hear you,' I said.

★ ★ ★

Soon after this conversation, a large pickup truck with flashing lights turned onto

214

Mildred Street. I could hear loud rap music as the passenger door opened and deposited Evian, a bit disheveled, on the sidewalk. The truck roared away. Evian came inside and said, 'I am really tired.' She threw herself onto the couch, her head inches from mine. She stretched and yawned theatrically.

I practiced the words in my head: *I need to take you home now.* But when I opened my mouth, I said, 'Do you want some spaghetti?'

'No,' she said, 'I'm good.'

'Do you have any homework?' I asked.

She laughed. 'No,' she said. Evian smelled like beer.

My phone rang. It was Camilla, from next door. 'Is everything okay over there?' she asked. 'I wasn't sure you were all right.'

'I'm fine,' I said. 'Don't worry about me.'

I hung up the phone. Evian fell asleep with her head on my shoulder. A new episode of *House Hunters International* began. A Canadian couple was looking for a Costa Rican bungalow in which they could begin a new life.

33

Carla

I ran toward the shelter, pushing the metal door open and finding a dim room full of slumbering people. The room smelled like unwashed skin. I scanned the bodies but did not see my brother. A priest who had been reading in the light provided by a small window stood and approached me. 'You are safe,' he said soothingly, quietly. 'God has brought you to this place, and you are safe.'

Terror burns your skin from the inside. Constant watchfulness freezes your bones. Looking at the kindly priest, I almost fell to the floor. My shoulders slid down my back, and I took a shuddering breath. 'Are you hungry?' he asked. I said nothing.

'Come,' said Father, and I followed him to a small kitchen where he ladled soup into a white bowl. He handed me the soup and I ate. 'Where have you come from?' he asked me.

'Tegucigalpa,' I said.

'And you are going to El Norte?'

'I am going to find my mother in Texas.'

He nodded. 'You are all alone?' he asked.

'I was with my brother, Junior. And another boy, Ernesto.' I described them both, and Father told me to stand. 'We have a soccer field in the back,' he said.

I was eager to get outside, but Father touched my arm and asked if I would like to have confession. Too afraid to admit the way I had been violated, I shook my head.

'Bad things happen to good people sometimes,' said Father. He placed his hand on my cheek. 'God forgives you, if your heart is good.' I wanted to believe Father. I looked deep into his brown eyes, searching.

'My heart,' I said.

He nodded. 'I know,' he said. 'God bless you, my child. You are a strong person to make this journey.'

On his face, I saw pity. I knew he had seen terrible things, worse, perhaps, than the ones I had seen. He knew — as I did now — about what was possible. We had both tasted evil.

Father took my hand. If I spoke, I would beg him to keep me, to be not just a priest but *my* father. I could stay here in this place, cleaning and cooking for others. If he would never let go of me, I would do anything.

We went to the back of the room where so many were sleeping. By the door, a large map was taped to the wall. I stopped short and

217

stared. I had seen maps in books when I had gone to school. Father put his finger on a city by the bottom of the map. 'Tegu,' he said. I watched him. He moved his hand up the map. 'And now you are here,' he said.

'And Texas?' I said.

Five inches higher, he touched a blue ribbon. 'The Rio Bravo,' he said. 'And if you cross it, you are in the United States.'

It didn't seem impossible, standing in that room, looking at a piece of paper. I'd come so far already. I thought for one moment about how it would feel to put my face into my mother's hair.

'You could go back,' said Father, mistaking my quiet for fear.

I shook my head.

'Your hope,' said Father. 'It inspires me, your hope.'

I was iridescent, empowered by his words. 'What else can I do but hope?' I asked. I assumed he knew what things were like at home.

'Indeed,' said Father.

I pushed open the back door, and there he was. He was bouncing a half-deflated ball, wearing only a pair of athletic shorts. I ran to Junior. 'I found you,' I cried.

'Ah, we're in the middle of a game,' he said, pushing me away but smiling large. His hair was clean and his eyes looked less dull than I remembered. To the other boys, Junior said, 'Keep playing. It's just my sister.'

34

Alice

Donn's Depot Piano Bar & Saloon had originally been an actual train station. When the wooden structure was slated to be replaced with a brick building, the older station was moved to Austin and attached to a boxcar, parlor car, and red caboose (the last now the ladies' room). Surrounded by an outdoor deck, the building was soon filled with the musical stylings of Austin native Donn Adelman, who'd bought the place in 1978. Donn and the Station Masters played live music on the weekends, and on weeknights you could never be sure if you'd be hearing a new band, an old band, or your personal jukebox selections. I always brought quarters in my purse, just in case. Parking was a bit of an issue, as West Fifth had become snazzy — full of spas, fitness studios, and something called a Blo Dry Bar. Behind the Depot, I wedged my car into a space uncomfortably close to a telephone pole and slithered out. It was happy hour, and the lot was almost full already.

I climbed the wooden steps to the deck and entered the bar. As always, the place was lit with Christmas lights. Though you couldn't smoke indoors anymore, the scent lingered. Marion sat near the empty stage with a drink. I waved and went to the bar, where Toni said, 'Alice!' and came forward to give me a big hug. I hadn't been to Donn's in two years.

'Hey,' I said happily.

'Where's the big guy, the famous one?' said Toni.

The young man behind the bar leaned in. 'Who's famous?' he said.

'This one's hubby. Conroe's BBQ!' said Toni.

'Whoa,' said the man, who sported a reddish goatee.

'She's famous, too,' said Toni kindly.

'I'll have a glass of Chardonnay,' I said.

'You can't come in here wearing those boots and order a Chardonnay,' said the man.

'She can do what she likes,' said Toni, unscrewing a large bottle and filling a pint glass to the rim with wine. I opened my purse, but Toni said, 'We'll run a tab,' shooing me away.

Marion stood as I approached. 'What *is* that?' she said.

'Chardonnay.'

'Ugh, in a beer glass?' said Marion. 'You've

got to try the Loose Caboose.'

'Sounds good.' I sat down at the rickety table, took a sip of my wine, and sighed. 'I need some advice,' I said.

'From me?' said Marion. She laughed. 'You need advice and I need a miracle.'

'What do you mean?'

'Oh, hon,' said Marion, smoothing her cocktail napkin. 'I've got this one school year to raise the TAKS scores and attendance records. One year, and then they close Chávez Memorial. To be honest, I think they're going to close us anyway.'

'What about the teachers?'

'What about the *kids?*' said Marion. She rubbed her eyes. 'I tell them I believe in them. I tell them I *love* them. I tell them I'm proud of them. But when — sorry. *If* they close Chávez, these kids are going to be in big trouble. Some of them won't even go to school anymore. Some of these kids' parents went to Chávez. Well, it wasn't called Chávez then, but my point is there used to be pride.' She sighed deeply. 'The teachers will find jobs. Maybe in Austin, maybe not. I'll find a job. But the kids . . . ' She stopped talking and drained her Loose Caboose.

'So Evian has moved in with me . . . with us,' I began.

'What?' said Marion, leaning toward me.

222

She wore a gold pin on her sweater — a Chávez jaguar.

'Her mom . . . she kicked her out, I guess.'

'Go on,' said Marion in a grim tone.

'I don't know what to do. Jake is angry. He says . . . I don't know, that we need some time to recover. I guess he thinks I'm replacing Mitchell with Evian. Or something. But I'm just trying to give her a safe place to live. Someone watching out for her.'

'My husband left me, my third year as principal,' said Marion. She raised her hand and Toni began fixing another drink. 'He told me I was married to the school. He wanted me home at night, to make dinner, to hear about his day. But there were basketball games, teacher meetings . . . there were kids who needed me, and I wanted to be there for them, the way their parents weren't, sometimes. Graham was an adult. When I saw some kid who needed to talk, I knew whom God would want me to help. I prayed every time Graham threatened to leave. And every time, God told me what my purpose was.' She shrugged, accepted the drink from Toni with a smile. 'But then Graham left,' she said.

'You're amazing,' I said.

'And I'm alone,' said Marion.

'Doesn't look like you will be for long,' I said, eyeing the older men in the bar, many wearing cowboy hats and Wranglers.

'I'm not alone *every* night,' said Marion. She winked. 'But in a larger sense,' she clarified, shrugging.

'What do you think I should do?' I asked.

'Honey, I can't answer that for you,' said Marion. Toni brought another pint of wine and placed it on the table. As I drank, I felt warm and confused. Toni took my empty glass away. Donn and the Station Masters took the stage and Marion and I listened, rapt and relaxed. Couples in their seventies and eighties took to the floor, two-stepping elegantly. A few younger hipsters moseyed out, and the elders revolved around them gracefully. A man with a bushy white moustache walked toward our table, his eyes fixed on Marion. 'Oh, boy,' she said sotto voce. 'Here we go.'

'Lovely Marion,' said the man, removing his hat.

'Hello, Clive,' said Marion.

'Would you do me the honor, darling?' said Clive. But as Marion was nodding, placing her hand in Clive's, her phone buzzed.

'Forgive me,' she said, glancing down at the text. Her face went cold. 'Oh, God,' she said. 'Oh, no.'

'Marion!' said Clive, alarmed.

'There's been a shooting,' said Marion. She

stood, flustered, gathering her purse. 'Gang-related, a football player . . . ' she said. 'Can you — '

'Of course,' I said. I stood and Marion hugged me quickly.

'Ask God what you should do,' she said as she hurried off. 'Don't ask me.'

Toni approached, and I told her what had happened. 'Forget it,' she said when I asked for the bill. 'Poor Marion.'

I sighed, slipping my purse over my shoulder.

'She tell you about the gym?' said Toni.

'What?' I said.

'Condemned,' said Toni. 'Marion's been in here, trying to convince Donn to hold the Chávez Homecoming Dance here in a few weeks. No way, Donn said, absolutely no way. Some of those kids are hoodlums, you know what.'

'I guess so,' I said. I made my way to my car, but it had become trapped between the telephone pole and a minivan. I sighed and began walking along 5th Street. It was only a few blocks to Lamar, where I could grab a cab. I was feeling kind of drunk anyway, and kind of sorry for myself.

The corner of Lamar and Fifth was bright with the giant Whole Foods flagship store. Dazed, drawn like a moth to a flame, I wandered inside. The entire store gleamed, even the customers — their hair shone, their teeth were pearls, sleek fabrics covered their trim limbs. The food was beautiful, lush and swollen. I felt as if I were in a dream of some futuristic, perfect place. The grains were lined up in alphabetical order, not a smudge on their Plexiglas containers. Rows of multicolored sushi gleamed, as perfect as untouched children's toys in their packaging. There was a wood-fired pizza station, a nut-roasting station, a fish counter with no fishy odor, and even a chocolate fountain, for the love of God! It was sickening. It was glorious. A place where every desire could be sated. I stood in the middle of the store and looked skyward, seeking understanding, but all I could see were more floors, escalators leading more wealthy people to limitless delights.

A woman in spandex pants bumped into me, knocking me off-balance. 'What the hell is the matter with you?' she said, her eyes frowning but her brow remaining shiny and uncreased. Under one arm, she held a firmly rolled yoga mat.

'I don't know,' I said truthfully.

'Maybe you should figure that out,' she said.

'Yes, I should,' I answered.

'In the meantime,' she added, 'maybe you

could move away from the gluten-free cookie bar.'

I nodded dumbly and stumbled out of the store. Back on Lamar, I felt a bit more like myself. I wanted, more than anything, to go back to Mildred Street and to have Jake there, asleep on the couch in his bathing suit. I ran back toward Donn's, and when I reached the parking lot, the minivan that had been blocking me was gone. It felt like a sign.

35

Carla

We spent almost a week in the shelter, planning how we would reach Texas. We shared stories and warnings, eating soup for three meals a day. Ernesto began romancing an older Mexican woman, whose brother, Marcos, had a job waiting for him in America. Marcos, stocky in a dark blue shirt and a hat that said 'No Fear,' took pity on us. Marcos had instructed his wife to mail money to him at various points in the journey, so he could not be robbed. In fact, he boasted, he planned to hire a *combi* from the shelter to Mexico City, bypassing a week or so on The Beast.

I began to follow Marcos like a puppy, it is true. It was amazing to think that he had an employer in America. There was even a Dodge Ram truck stashed for him in Laredo, Texas! The owner of a farm had given Marcos the truck when it became too old for his use, Marcos told me. He liked to boast, but I was happy to listen. I had never known a father, much less a handsome one with money and a job. I sat at his feet while he told stories. And I was not the only one!

Marcos and his brothers, he said, traveled every year from Southern Mexico to Texas. For eight years now he'd been riding the rails, picking up the Dodge Ram in a parking lot just over the border, then driving it to the farm. Marcos had no map but knew the roads by heart, especially the ones to avoid because of border agents. 'We are such good workers, we are worth a Dodge Ram,' said Marcos proudly. His three brothers smiled and nodded, a bit more bashful but not much more bashful. After the harvest, they returned home for Christmas, bearing lavish gifts and money. The following year, they headed north again.

'This year we brought our sister, Juliana,' said Marcos. 'If she marries that young friend of yours, the rancher will be very happy with me.'

I was surprised Marcos thought a boy with a number tattooed on his face would be a good match, but I guess muscles are muscles at harvest-time. Marcos scrutinized my expression. 'Is he a good man?' asked Marcos.

'He helps me and my brother out of kindness,' I said.

Marcos nodded, pleased. 'My sister made a bad choice in Xaltianguis,' he mused, 'but maybe this friend of yours can turn her life around. Would he be a good father?'

I swallowed. 'He has been like a father to me and my brother,' I chirped. I hoped God would forgive me for stretching the truth.

Marcos nodded, impressed.

'We were alone in Tegucigalpa,' I added, unable to stop talking. 'Ernesto found us without food. My grandmother had died. Out of the goodness of his heart, he offered to help us find our mother.'

Marcos listened, and having him pay attention to me was like a drug.

'He . . . he found us food. He protected us as best he could. He is . . . like an uncle to me.'

The dinner bell rang, and Marcos looked away.

'He's in love with Juliana, I can see!' I blurted. But Marcos was already walking into the large kitchen, where Father was ladling soup. I scrambled after him.

For those of us who did not have the fortune it would cost to hire a *combi*, the train from Ixtapec through northern Veracruz and toward Mexico City was rumored to be especially dangerous; we were in a valley of lawlessness (explained Father) where unsavory characters lay in wait to steal from us, violate us, and kidnap or kill us. Father did not treat me like a child, which I appreciated, because I no longer felt like a child.

I lay awake on my cardboard bed at night, going over the route in my mind, tracing the lines that led from Ixtapec to Nuevo Laredo and the Rio Bravo (called the Rio Grande on the map). Next to me, Junior slept, his breath shallow. I knew he was still sniffing Resistol. He left the shelter in the afternoons and returned with a vacant stare and little appetite. I told him that he was risking his life, venturing from the shelter, but he ignored me, so I stopped scolding. The power of the glue was far stronger than my words. I had decided to believe that the shifty-eyed boy who cared more for fumes than his sister was a devil who was inhabiting my brother. I had seen Father looking at him warily. I had to get Junior to our mother, I knew, so she could take care of us. I prayed for his recovery, though I could not think of anyone who had come back from the place Junior had gone.

★ ★ ★

The day before they were leaving in the *combi*, Marcos and his brothers told me, Ernesto, and Junior that they would allow us to ride with them. At the thought of

231

bypassing a week on The Beast, of sleeping in a van instead of facing the sickening lurching, exhaustion, and terror of the train, I began to weep. 'Do not cry, little bird,' said Marcos, putting his warm palm on the top of my head. 'God is good.'

Junior remained expressionless.

In the yard where we played with the limp soccer ball, I told Junior that an inch in the *combi* was priceless — a chance to stay alive for another leg of the journey! Of course, the driver could be dishonest: he could drive us to a secluded spot and rob or kill us. But Marcos seemed to know what he was doing. 'You can sit on my lap,' I told Junior. 'You can sleep without fear. We have been blessed!'

Junior didn't seem to hear me. He scanned the playground for something more, something else, something I didn't have to give.

The night before our departure, I could not sleep. Marcos had said we would leave before dawn. I thanked God for saving me from having to climb on the train again. I knew the *combi* route was dangerous, marked with immigration checkpoints, but nothing scared me as much as The Beast, and the things that could happen to a girl on The Beast at night.

Endless minutes later, I heard Ernesto's voice. 'Wake up, Carla,' he said. 'We're leaving now.'

I sat up, rubbing my face. I put my hand out, groping for my brother's bony shoulder.

'Come, child,' said Father. 'I will bless you all together before you depart.'

There was no bony shoulder. 'Where's Junior?' I whispered. I stood and went outside. The *combi* idled, surrounded by Marcos and his family. Ten of us would fit like an awkward jigsaw puzzle into the van. In the coal-colored night, I searched for Junior.

'God be with you,' began Father. His voice was warm honey. He told us that his blessing was from the families we had left behind, from the mothers and fathers and children we were going to El Norte to assist. He said the prayers were for those who had come before us, and for those who would soon arrive. We bowed our heads and thanked God for our lives, for God's love and guidance. Father concluded, and I saw Ernesto put his arms around Juliana, holding her under the low sky. Maybe he did love her; who knew? Hand in hand, they walked toward the truck.

Ernesto remembered me and looked back. 'Carla,' he said. 'Come. It's time.'

'What about my brother?' I said. No one answered. We all knew Junior was seeking glue. The driver pressed his foot to the gas pedal, making the engine hum.

'God be with you,' said Father.

I was rooted to the ground. To get into the van would be to abandon Junior. It was the hardest decision I had made until this point. I thought about the lurching of The Beast. I thought about my hands, frozen solid, on the hopper rails. I thought about the man with the wolf eyes who had made me into a woman without my consent, how it had felt to be split apart.

'Carla,' said Marcos, 'come, child. We must go.' The *combi* door remained open. The bodies of my companions, none of them my relative by blood, would be warm.

There is no other way to say it: I chose myself.

36

Alice

I drove past the Whole Foods, across the interstate, to the Eastside. I parked in front of our house, ran up the walk, and threw open my door. Jake was nowhere to be seen. Instead, Evian and Sam were entwined in front of our television, watching *House Hunters International* and dry humping.

'Break it up!' I shouted. They separated quickly, Sam sitting up and putting his glasses on, Evian glaring at me sultrily, her lipstick smeared. 'One of Sam's friends was *shot* tonight,' said Evian defiantly. 'And you are *not* going to tell me we can't hang out and help each other *process*!'

'In fact, yes, I am,' I said. 'I'm sorry, Sam, but you need to go home now. And Evian, so do you.'

Sam rose, murmured goodbye, and hustled out the door. Evian glared at me. 'Someone shot our friend,' she cried. She crossed her arms across her unbuttoned shirt.

'Evian, we need to talk,' I said. I sat down on the couch, and she turned her back to me.

On the television, a man said, 'They call this a bedroom?' I picked up the remote and turned it off.

'Listen,' I said. 'I want to help you. But you can't live here anymore. I'm going to take you home to your mom now.'

Evian turned to face me. Instead of screaming or protesting, she seemed resigned. She sighed. 'Okay,' she said.

★   ★   ★

The usual dogs rushed my car as we drove toward Evian's trailer. I shuddered. 'They're *dogs*,' said Evian nastily.

The trailer was filled with light, and when I stopped the car, a woman with dark hair came outside. She looked exhausted. I took a breath, prepared to open my door. But Evian leapt from the car and ran into her mother's arms. They held each other, then went inside the trailer. I was unsure about what I should do. Evian had surprised me more than once already.

Slowly, I got out of the car and gathered Evian's things. The dogs barked at me as I piled them outside the door. Before leaving, I called, 'Bye!'

Evian opened the front door. 'Um, Ms. Conroe?' she said. 'Thanks.'

Evian's mother appeared. 'I appreciate you keeping an eye on this wild thing,' she said. 'I do.'

'Okay,' I said. 'Well, goodbye.'

I drove away feeling as if something in me had been scraped out. It seemed strange that no one was mad at me — not Evian, for returning her home; not her mother, for letting her stay with me. The truth was painful to admit — I didn't matter all that much to either of them. As I stopped at a red light on South First, my phone buzzed with a message from Evian: *Can u take me to mall this wknd to get dress for Homecoming???*

I texted back: *You got it.*

⋆ ⋆ ⋆

Jake's truck was parked on Mildred. Happiness flooded my body at the sight of it. I heard Beau's voice as I parked the car, and found Jake, Beau, and Camilla in our backyard. 'Honey!' said Jake, his face alight at the sight of me.

'Honey,' I answered.

'We brought margaritas,' said Beau.

'The girls are asleep,' said Camilla. 'I have the baby monitor in one hand and a margarita in the other. Is this bad parenting?'

'I don't think so,' said Beau, touching her

hair. We only had three porch chairs, so I sank into Jake's lap. He put his arms on either side of me. I was home.

37

Carla

The *combi* drove all night, and I tried to sleep. Although I was more tired than I had ever been, I stared out the window, unable to rest. We took back roads. At one point in the journey, we stopped to relieve ourselves. My eyes and mouth felt caked with sand. The night smelled of sage. I wondered if Junior had returned to the shelter. I tried to comprehend that I would never see him again.

After a few minutes, the driver said, 'Get back inside.'

Marcos and his brothers filed quickly into the *combi*. They were professionals: sleeping every instant it was possible, completely alert and ready to run in a fraction of a second if necessary. I moved reluctantly. My brain was not well — I considered walking back down the road, finding Junior and telling him he was mistaken: I was not the kind of person who could leave her brother behind.

'Carla!' said Ernesto.

I stood and crammed myself into the

combi. I was more afraid of the darkness than I was of becoming a stranger to myself.

★ ★ ★

When the sky was lavender, the *combi* dropped us in an alley near the train station. In Mexico City, the farthest north I had ever been, I looked heavenward and gave thanks. I was still alive.

I knew I should feel elated to have made it out of Chiapas. I was one more train ride from the United States border. But leaving my brother had given me an illness. Around me, my friends were in good spirits, but I felt achy and exhausted. Marcos told us to be patient and wait for the correct train, which would take us to Nuevo Laredo, located across the Rio Bravo from Laredo, Texas. 'I have no Dodge Ram in California!' he said. 'A train bound for Tijuana or Nogales does nothing for me!'

Now that I had failed my brother, I began to feel that my journey was without value. If I showed myself to *la migra*, told them I was Honduran, I would be sent on the so-called Bus of Tears to Tegucigalpa. I would not be crying, however. I would be thinking of Humberto and the life we could begin. We would not have much for food, and there was

240

the smell of the dump, but even so, it was heaven on earth compared to Mexico City.

The harsh morning illuminated ugly Lechería Station. I looked at the violent graffiti (Jesus stabbed with a knife, for example, or a gun against the head of a child) and knew that evil people watched us, waiting to see what they could take. My will to move forward was small. I was afraid.

In a shop window, I saw myself for the first time since I had left Tegu. My eye was swollen and ringed in bluish brown where I had been hit on the train. A large cut — almost healed — had left a scar on my cheek. I was so skinny you could see the bones beneath my face. I looked like a starving mongrel. I stared at the glass. What had I become?

★　★　★

We spent a night by the tracks, and still the correct train did not arrive. It felt like a sign. I had forsaken my brother and I hated myself. I watched the dirty sky through eyes covered in grit. What was the point of this?

Finally, my head on discarded newspaper, I dreamed. I thought of Humberto — his arms, his hands, and his lips. He would not have to know I had been raped on the train. I could

241

never tell him of my shame — I would be cast out of my village if anyone knew, and Humberto, much as he loved me, could never make a good life with me, marrying (as we had planned) in Maria Auxiliadora Church.

But there was no one to tell him, now that Junior was lost. I could stand at the altar in a white wedding gown. I felt that God would forgive me. And when Humberto touched my body, it would be healed.

I woke with a feeling that there was something left for me. I found Ernesto next to Juliana and told him I was going back to Tegu. 'Why, when we are so close?' he asked.

'I'm sick,' I said. 'I need to go home.'

Juliana put her cool hand on my forehead. She shook her head. 'No fever,' she said. Her eyes were kind. 'Don't you understand?' she said.

'Understand what?' I said.

'Carla,' said Ernesto, 'we have no home.'

38

Alice

For the first weeks of September, life was wonderfully ordinary. When I woke in the morning, Jake had gone to Conroe's and Pete was curled up in his place. We went for walks around Lady Bird Lake or just to work, passing Chávez Memorial and waving at whoever was outside smoking or watching the smokers. Grupo told me the injured student was recovering at St. David's. He'd been shot in the leg and was expected to be fine, though he wouldn't play football for a while. The shooting had been gang-related, and when the Gang Prevention Task Force came in on Wednesday evenings, I served them the best brisket, which I'd set aside.

Marion was stopping kids in the hallways, she said, making them change their gang-colored shirts, dragging them into her office and handing them tees she'd gotten from Goodwill and Savers. Jake gave her a few boxes of Conroe's shirts, and we got a kick out of seeing students walk by with our logo on their chests. The girls wore the XXLs belted with leggings.

As Homecoming — always held on the first weekend of October — approached, Marion presided over meetings late into the night. She stopped by our house some evenings, staying for a beer and telling us how conflicted she felt. 'On the one hand,' she said, picking at her Shiner label, 'it's just stupid to go ahead with the Homecoming football game. And the dance. It's dangerous. A big fat invitation to disaster.'

'That's true,' said Jake.

'On the other hand,' said Marion, 'what do these kids have to look forward to? Some of them won't graduate. Only a very few will go to college. This weekend — it's the best night for some of them.'

'Good point,' said Jake. He looked wistful, and after Marion left and we lay on the couch, I ran my fingers through his hair. 'Was Homecoming your best time?' I asked gingerly.

'Of course not,' he said, clasping my hand. 'But you never feel things so deeply — so strongly — as you do in high school. You know?'

'I guess,' I said. I couldn't have cared less about Homecoming — Ouray High didn't have a football team. I remembered hiking Mount Sneffels by myself instead of going to the school dance, trying to get closer to my mom somehow by getting higher, by going to one of her favorite spots (albeit one she'd forbidden me to climb to alone — or at night). It hadn't worked, and I'd made my way down freezing cold, hating her for leaving me, vowing never to let myself be such a sucker again.

'We played Del Valle,' said Jake. His voice was far away. 'It was a close game, and in the last quarter I fucked up.'

'I'm sure you didn't,' I said.

'It was a series of fuck-ups, but we didn't play like we could have. I caught a pass and tried to run it, trying to be the big shot. I should have passed the ball, but I ran, and this big guy brought me right down. I blew it.'

'That was a long time ago,' I said.

'I still feel like an ass about it,' said Jake. 'And my girlfriend at the time, Francine LePour, she got really drunk at the after-party and I had to hold her hair back while she puked.'

He looked up at me, and I was surprised to see how upset he'd become. 'It's all over now,' I said. 'Everything's fine now, honey.'

Jake sat up. 'I'm not asking you to fix it,' he said sharply. 'I'm just saying it sucked. Can you listen to me, for once?'

Tears sprang to my eyes. 'I don't

245

understand what's wrong,' I said.

'I just feel like — ' Jake began. My phone buzzed, and he stopped talking. He met my eyes. The phone rang again. I picked it up and saw that it was Jane's husband, who had never called me before. 'It's Dennis,' I said.

Jake shook his head, made a disappointed sound in his throat. He stood and went into our room. Pete followed, climbing into his crate at the foot of the bed. Jake shut the bedroom door with more force than was necessary.

'Dennis?' I said, answering my phone. 'What's going on?'

'Hi,' said my brother-in-law. 'Listen, I . . . it's bad news. I'm calling with bad news. I wanted to let you know . . . well, we lost the baby.'

'Oh, no,' I said. 'Oh, Dennis, no.'

'It happens sometimes,' said Dennis. 'But Jane's taking it hard. I just thought you ought to know.'

'When did this happen?' I asked. 'What can I do?'

'Night before last.' Dennis sighed heavily. 'Jane started bleeding and just . . . it wasn't meant to be. The doctor said there was probably something wrong with the baby. It's early — this just happens sometimes.'

'Why didn't you call me?'

'It's been crazy, Alice,' said Dennis. 'Jane just got home a few hours ago.'

'I'm coming,' I said. 'I'll get a flight out tonight.'

'I don't think that's necessary,' said Dennis.

'I'll call when I land,' I said.

'I don't mean to be . . . ' Dennis stopped, sighed again. 'Listen,' he said, 'Jane said to tell you she'll call you when she wakes up. You don't need to come here. To be frank, we could use some time as a family.'

'I am family,' I said, booting up the laptop.

'You know what I mean,' said Dennis.

'Okay, I'll see you soon,' I said, hanging up the phone.

After a short Internet search, I booked a flight to Denver. I'd arrive by morning, and could deal with getting to Ouray from there. It was a six-hour drive; I could rent a car or grab a flight to Montrose. I thought about waking Jake, to tell him what had happened, and what I felt I should do. But I was afraid of him telling me I should wait, call Jane in the morning. I didn't want to hear about how I had to stand by, feel my feelings, *process*. Moving simply felt better than being still.

I tossed a few things in a bag, went into the kitchen, and jotted a note on the pad we used for grocery lists. Then I called Austin Taxi and headed out.

39

Carla

Marcos led us from the Nuevo Laredo train station along a wavering path to a bank of reeds, beyond which was a campground. From the campground, I could see America. The enormous river was all that separated me from my mother and my second brother, Carlos. The only ones in the world who *had* to love me were just across the water. Unhappily, the Rio Bravo was guarded by men in gleaming SUVs, men equipped with cameras, spotlights, even helicopters. Keeping me — and all those like me — out of America was an important operation, I could see. I felt despised, a cockroach.

We arrived at nightfall. The campground smelled of shit. It was full of drug addicts, goats, thieves, and migrants hoping to enter the United States. Marcos insisted it was safer here than in the city, which was full of *la migra* and every other sort of problem and depravity.

Marcos would leave in the morning — he had the money to pay a *coyote* to get him over the river and past the immigration authorities. He would bring along his family, and perhaps Ernesto. But this place, with the soiled mattresses and trash, was where I would remain. At the edge of the trail, I leaned over and tried to throw up. There was nothing inside me, but still I heaved.

We sat around a campfire. In the middle of an awful place, the flames were hot and beautiful. I stared at them. I held my hands out. Marcos explained the ways to get into America. You could try to swim the river, but you would drown. He had seen bloated bodies float past in the water; he had seen people stopped halfway across by American police, then put in jail, then sent back to the country they had started in. Even as we sat by the fire, people were trying to make it through the rushing water. INS agents with bullhorns stood on the far shore, telling the swimmers to turn back in both English and Spanish. It was like having a campout in the middle of one of the action movies we used to watch through the window of the PriceSmart electronics store. I imagined that the loud, disembodied voices were Bruce Willis and Arnold Schwarzenegger (who had also been an immigrant, I knew). The idea made me smile. It is helpful to pretend a horrifying scenario is not your real life.

Marcos said that some rode inner tubes to a resting place covered in vegetation, an island in the middle of the water, halfway to America. They waited there, sometimes all night, for a split second when they were not watched. If that moment came, they might make it across. 'But then they are on a muddy bank in wet clothes, surrounded by police! This is stupid, and it is foolish, though your hopes will tell you otherwise.'

Marcos knew what he was talking about, and I nodded. Across the water I could see American houses. I could hear cars at the border checkpoint. I was so close, and Marcos was right: a part of my brain said, *Just go, Carla! Just swim across!*

'There is a Catholic church in Nuevo Laredo,' Marcos continued. He told me how to get there — it was not too long a walk from the camp. 'At the church, you will get food cards worth fifteen meals,' said Marcos. 'Are you listening, Carla?'

I turned to him, the man who had helped me so much already. I took a breath, then made my plea. 'Please,' I said. 'Take me with you.'

He shook his head sadly, impatiently. 'My employer pays our fee to the *coyote*,' he explained. 'He takes it from my first paycheck. If you are not coming as a laborer, he will not pay for you. Juliana will cook for us while we are there, and if Ernesto wants to work very hard, he can join us.'

Ernesto looked up, wonder in his eyes. He looked younger than the day I had met him. He was smitten, I saw now, if not with Juliana, then with her family. He had someone besides a gang to love him now.

'Is there something I can do there, in Texas?' I asked, desperate not to be left at this place on my own. In the firelight, I saw waves of red ants along the ground, the kind that sting.

'Listen to me,' said Marcos. 'I will introduce you to the *coyote* — he is trustworthy. I have used him before. He knows the way across, and he has contacts to get us to the truck. He costs two thousand U.S. dollars a person, but he will not take the money and leave you dead.'

'How will I get two thousand dollars?' I asked.

'You will call your mother,' said Marcos. Solemnly he whispered, 'Give me your hand.'

Marcos was sitting next to me. When I let my hand near his, he put a card inside and closed my fingers around it. 'You are in danger now,' he said very quietly. 'You have a possession many others want. Use this as soon as it is light. Tell your mother to wire the money before your fifteen meals run out.'

I nodded, too frightened to speak.

I felt surrounded by menace from that moment on. We had no food, so did not eat. I lay down on a soiled blanket near the fire. I did not open my hand. Sometime in the night I felt a kiss on my forehead. I sat up, terrified, but it was Ernesto.

'Adios, Carla,' he said. He knelt by my side.

'Ernesto,' I said, 'please. Don't tell anyone what happened to me on the train.'

He nodded seriously. 'I promise,' he said.

'Do you love Juliana?' I asked.

'We are leaving,' he said.

In the shadows, I could see Juliana, Marcos, and their brothers. Beside them was a very thin man with a beard. 'This is El Serpiente,' said Marcos, approaching. 'You will pay him when your money arrives. Until then, he will keep you safe.'

I was too scared to respond. I cowered on the blanket. The Snake lit a cigarette and said, 'Marcos, let's go.' They followed him along the water, out of sight. I could sense men watching me, and I felt sick.

It was not yet morning, but I stood up anyway. I ran the way I had come, up the path, to the city. I ran for maybe an hour, maybe longer. Finally, I collapsed on a bench and opened my hand to see that Marcos had given me a phone card worth fifty pesos. I saw an old woman walking quickly down the dark street and I asked her where a phone was. She looked at me as if she, too, were afraid. I knew that some migrants were not kind, and robbed or stole to get what they needed to survive. The old woman shook her head and hurried away.

I found the church Marcos had told me about, and on its steps I curled into a ball to wait for morning. I had come so far, and I did not know what to do. I knew I was in danger. I knew my mother might not have the money. And I knew she might not send it; she had left me, after all. Did she love me two thousand dollars' worth?

The good news here is that I had no more tears left. So I sat on the steps of Parroquia de San José until God brought the morning to me.

40

Alice

As soon as I stepped off the plane in Montrose, I could feel the chill of impending winter. It was only September, and yet the light was low and gray, the sky steely outside the airport windows. In the baggage claim, my father waited, his summer tan worn off, his expression miserable. When he saw me, he nodded, unsmiling. I ran to him, saying, 'Dad,' as I tucked my arms underneath his and held him.

'Come on now, honey,' he said, disengaging himself.

At the baggage carousel, he leaned in to grab my duffel. 'I can do it,' I protested, but he ignored me. We walked across the parking lot. Montrose was flat, and the sky seemed stretched too thin to cover the distance from the clouds to asphalt. My father started the truck. 'Chilly,' I commented.

He did not respond.

'How's Jane?' I tried.

'Better today,' he said. 'She'll be fine.'

'I wish she'd get the test,' I said. 'The test

for the gene that . . . ' My voice trailed off. I couldn't say the word: *cancer*.

'Got a new boy in the stockroom,' said my father. 'Bill Fernandez's boy.'

'Oh,' I said. 'How's he doing?'

'Fine,' Dad said with a shrug. He turned on the radio, found a country-western station. We drove the forty-five minutes to Ouray without a word. 'You staying with Jane or me or what?' Dad asked as we pulled into town.

'I don't know,' I said. He did not respond. 'Jane, I guess,' I said.

Dad pulled up in front of Jane's house and parked, carrying my duffel to her door, then gathering groceries from the backseat. 'What's in the bags?' I asked.

'Jane likes those Sara Lee pound cakes,' said my father. He let himself inside Jane's quiet house, put the cakes on the kitchen counter, kissed me on the cheek, and left.

Dennis had left a note saying that he and the children were at the store and that Jane was resting. I called for her. When she did not reply, I climbed upstairs. My sister was in bed, her hair unwashed and greasy on the pillow. I lay down next to her, and she turned to face me.

'Hi,' I said.

'Hi,' said Jane. She started to cry. 'I'm really sad,' she said.

'I know,' I said.

'You do know,' said Jane. 'I'm sorry for being sad.'

'You don't have to be sorry,' I said.

Jane nodded, still crying, and closed her eyes. This was how we'd bunked as children, in one bed. I brought my forehead close to my sister's, and we slept.

★　★　★

'Our names are so *plain*,' said Jane as we sat in bed that night, waiting for the boys and Dennis to bring us dinner. 'I mean, Jane and Alice? What could be more dull?'

'I don't know,' I said. 'I like my name.' I'd changed into pajamas and we'd settled in for a long evening of watching Lifetime Television for Women. Jane kept the volume low so she could talk over the movie, which was about a waitress in a seaside town who falls in love with the fry cook, who, unbeknownst to the waitress, is also a serial killer.

'I just feel like Mom and Dad could have branched out some,' said Jane, waving her mug around. I watched her hand nervously, waiting to get a scalding slap of Nighty Night tea.

'Jane and Alice were their mothers' names,' I said.

'That is my point!' said Jane, lifting her arm.

'Please,' I said, 'can you watch your hot mug there, sister?'

'You watch your hot mug, sister!' she said. She spoke gaily but also seemed a bit unhinged. I did not point out that I was drinking a mug of whiskey, which Dennis had handed me without comment.

'Dinner's ready!' called Rick, entering the room. He was so tall now, still thin as a rail, wearing athletic shorts though it was cold outside. It was strange to look at him — so sweet, grinning at his mom — and realize that he was just two years younger than Evian and the other Chávez kids, who seemed so world-weary. Rick's face, covered with pimples and rosy-colored from his culinary efforts, was open and trusting. I wondered if mine had ever been that way.

Part of me was glad to have learned the tough lesson early — life could take everything from you when you weren't paying attention. So I watched. Like the Chávez kids, I was ready for disappointment. But looking at Rick, I felt a hot jealousy. I yearned to feel at ease but didn't know how.

'Okay,' said Rick, his voice deeper than I remembered. 'We have your broccoli here.' He gestured to a bowl of overcooked greens with a pat of cold butter on top.

'Oh my God, amazing,' said Jane.

'And I carried the noodles,' piped up Gilmer. He tried to climb on the bed with a bowl of spaghetti, and spilled only some on the floor and in our laps. The strands were clumped together, half cooked and seemingly without sauce or flavoring of any kind.

'I love noodles!' said Jane. 'How did you know?'

'I brought the forks!' screamed Benjamin, throwing them in the air. We ducked, and the utensils landed safely at the foot of the bed. Jane reached for them and said, 'You are so smart to bring forks, Benji.' He beamed and began to jump in place.

'Last but not least,' said Dennis, entering, 'fresh trout.'

He placed a tray of fish, perfectly sautéed in garlic and butter, on the bedside table.

'Oh, man,' I said. 'This looks delicious.'

When the children had gone, Dennis shooing them out of the room so they would miss the scene of the fry cook stabbing someone on a beach, Jane said, 'He fishes every night now. It's how he copes.' She sighed, all her goodwill spent.

'Napkins!' screamed Gilmer, throwing a roll of paper towels from the hallway. 'I'm not allowed to come in!' he added.

With effort, Jane climbed from bed. She

went to the door and kissed her son. 'I was just asking Aunt Alice what we were going to do without napkins,' she said. Gilmer hugged her tight, clasping his pudgy hands together around her head.

'Gilmer! What'd I tell you?' Dennis thundered.

'Yikes, bye!' said Gilmer. Jane closed the door quietly and climbed back into bed.

'Who's up for trout?' I said.

Jane was motionless, her eyes closed. 'I'll be fine,' she said.

I was quiet. I ate dinner and watched the movie. I knew there was nothing I could do but be next to her. Dennis checked in about an hour later, whispering that he was headed out to have a drink at the Elks lodge. I walked him to the front door. 'Are you doing okay?' I asked, putting my hand on his arm.

Dennis squinted at the stars. I could tell it took force of will for him to keep from moving his arm away. 'Yup,' he said.

My dad's truck pulled up the road. 'You're going drinking with my dad?' I asked.

'Yup,' said Dennis, taking a can of Skoal from his jacket pocket.

My dad put the truck in park but left the car idling. 'Dennis?' he called.

'Yup,' said Dennis, heading down the stairs.

'Hi, Dad!' I called. He nodded, waited for Dennis to climb in, and drove off.

I sat on the front steps for a while. I went inside and found Jane's hidden stash of cigarettes just where she'd always kept it, in a basket atop the refrigerator. I went back outside and lit a cigarette. I took one inhale, feeling the false contentment nicotine always sent through my blood. Coughing, I put out the rest of the cigarette.

'Aunt Alice, you shouldn't smoke,' said Rick. I turned and saw him in the doorway, wearing a T-shirt and plaid pajama pants.

'Busted,' I said.

'Really,' said Rick. 'It's so bad for you.'

'You're right,' I said.

'So you know what happened to the baby?' said Rick.

I blinked, unsure of how to respond. 'What do you mean?' I said.

'There was something wrong with the baby,' said Rick. 'Sometimes that just happens.'

I nodded. 'Yeah,' I said.

'Nobody knows why,' said Rick.

I held his gaze, nodding. In his face, I saw a dim terror, the dawning understanding of how much he had to lose.

41

Carla

The priest, an old man in robes, took my crumpled phone card and let me use the church telephone. I dialed my mother's number carefully. Her phone rang once, and then again. On the third ring, she answered, '¿*Bueno?* Hello?'

'Mami?' I said.

'*Gracias a Dios!*' she shouted, so loud that the priest looked up and smiled. 'Carla, you are alive!'

'Yes!' I shouted, bursting into tears.

'Where are you?' she asked. 'I've called everyone! They told me you had gone!'

'Nuevo Laredo,' I said.

'Oh, baby,' she said, 'oh, my baby, you've almost made it.' The happiness in her voice made me cry louder. 'How on earth — '

'I need to get across the river,' I said. 'I need help. Two thousand dollars.'

She paused. I knew how much money this was to my mother, and I bit my tongue. Did she know what it was like in Nuevo Laredo? 'I'm scared,' I said, hoping she would understand about the campsite and the robbers and the children selling their bodies in the street. I did not say, *I am scared I will die*. But my mother had been here herself.

'You have found a *coyote?*' she said.

'Yes,' I said. 'I am told he is trustworthy. But he won't help me without money.'

'Of course,' she said. There was the smallest pause. 'I will send it today,' said my mother.

'Today?' I said, stunned. I quickly gave her the information necessary to send the money.

'You will be here tomorrow,' said my mother, her voice disbelieving. 'You will be here with me tomorrow!' she repeated.

'Thank you,' I said. 'Mami, my phone card is running out,' I said, panic rising in my chest.

'Precious one, be safe,' said my mother. In a smaller voice, she asked, 'And Junior?'

Tears rushed into my throat. I gagged on the words, but I spoke. 'No, Mami.'

There was no sound. My expensive seconds on the phone card ticked away as she tried to put unanswerable questions into words. I could hear my heart thudding in my ears. 'Junior . . . ?' she said again.

'I'm sorry,' I said.

Her silence expanded to form a terrible darkness over me. But finally my mother's voice broke through. 'Goodbye until tomorrow,' she said.

'Goodbye until tomorrow,' I whispered. I handed the phone to the priest.

★ ★ ★

The church was small and in bad repair. Above the pot of stew, Jesus Christ looked down on us from a large cross. The stew tasted so wonderful I had to hold it in my mouth before swallowing. I was very hungry. Around me were dozens of others, all starving, hollow-eyed. We were the lucky ones.

The priest had errands downtown, so he took me to the Western Union himself. He warned me that sometimes relatives promise to send money but do not. This was why he had to limit the meals he could give. 'Some people end up staying in Nuevo Laredo for a long time,' he said. He smiled mournfully. 'We do what we can do,' he said.

'Thank you,' I said.

He put his hand on my shoulder. 'Perhaps you will get there,' he said. 'Perhaps your American dream will come true, and it will be all you wished for.' He looked at me, hope in his eyes. 'It's possible, isn't it?' he said. He seemed to be asking himself this question.

At the Western Union, two thousand American dollars was waiting in my name. I stowed the money in my underwear, went with the priest back to the church for dinner, then brought the money to the encampment. When I found the Snake, he was not well. I understood his state: he looked like Junior after the Resistol. I asked him if my friends had made it over the border, and he said yes. For all I knew he had killed them all — who would ever discover his crimes? Still, I pulled the Western Union envelope from my pants and handed it to the Snake. 'Can you get me to Austin, Texas?' I asked. I told him my mother's address, which I had committed to memory.

He put the money in his back pocket and nodded lazily. 'We will leave soon,' he said. 'Make yourself comfortable, girl, and I will make arrangements.'

I was overcome. I did not believe him, yet I had no choice but to believe him. Though I knew vultures were watching, I lay on the soiled blanket, feeling sick but trying not to vomit. Finally it became dark. I heard the Snake departing, saying goodbye to those around the fire. I prayed, my eyes shut tight. I could not close my ears, however. I heard splashing and cries as the Rio Bravo ate those who tried to swim. I listened to the bullhorns as Bruce Willis and Arnold Schwarzenegger shouted, 'Go back! Go back!'

But I could not go back.

In the dead of night, the Snake shook me awake. Soundlessly we headed along a dirt path to a secluded place by the water. Night-blind, I could not see any American SUVs across the river. 'Climb on, quickly,' said the Snake, indicating a black inner tube he held still with his hand. Uncertainly, I mounted the tube. The Snake put a plastic bag with dry clothes in my lap. Then he launched us into the fierce river, trying to paddle forward, keeping the tube level so I would not tumble into the water. If I drowned, I realized, no one would tell my mother. I would just never arrive, and after a while she would understand.

I did as the Snake ordered, frozen with fear. We reached the island in the middle of the river and slid to safety. Mercifully, I did not see any agents on the American side. 'Don't make a sound,' said the Snake. 'Nothing.' I bit my tongue as he pushed us from the island back into the river. I was so close to America. Finally we reached the bank. The Snake hurried me along the land to a tributary. We followed it, the Snake watching our surroundings carefully. In the distance, a spotlight illuminated the island in the middle of the river. It was empty.

'Put on the dry clothes,' said the Snake, and I changed out of the pants and shirt I had worn for so long. The new pants were too tight, but the sweatshirt was large enough to cover where the zipper would not reach. There were shoes, too, and I tied them tightly. Shoes were of great value.

'Now,' whispered the Snake, 'we run.'

He began to sprint, and I fell in beside him. We ran for a long time, up from the river onto dirt trails behind a housing development. We crossed a paved road and saw a car ahead. The headlights blinked on and off. 'There,' said the Snake. We reached the car, and the Snake opened the trunk. 'Get in,' he said.

My mind reeled back in time, to the day I watched my baby brother being set in a trunk. Now, at last, it was me. But the space was small, and when the Snake slammed it shut, I did not have enough air. What if Marcos was wrong? What if I died here, in America, in a car trunk? The car started to move, stopping briefly at what I imagined were border checkpoints. I fell in and out of slumber.

By the time the trunk was opened, it was very hot. I gasped the fresh air and saw the sun. A stranger's face came into focus. He was a white man, an American, with gray hair and the stubble of a gray beard.

The strange man said, 'Get out.'

My legs were weak. I had vomited on myself, and the man wrinkled his nose. We were parked in front of a motel called the Ace. Faded cars shone under a brilliant sky. 'Room Sixteen?' said the man, reading to himself off a piece of paper. The Snake was gone.

I nodded.

The man dragged me to a red door that had the number sixteen spray-painted on its metal surface. Outside the door was a folding chair, an ashtray, and three empty cans of American beer. The man knocked sharply. The door was yanked open, and I saw her.

'*Mami!*' I said, falling toward her.

'Carla!' cried my mother, catching me.

42

Alice

Early in the morning, Jane shook me awake. 'Come on,' she said. 'I want to do Bridge of Heaven.'

'It's dark out,' I said. 'Are you sure you're up to it?'

'Please,' said Jane. 'I'm feeling strong. I . . . I need to do this.' The hike was at least a seven-hour round-trip, so I gritted my teeth and climbed from her cozy bed. 'I have coffee,' said Jane. 'Meet me in the Land Cruiser.' I nodded, half asleep. I changed into hiking clothes, shoved my hair under a hat, and brushed my teeth. None of the children were awake. Dennis lay on the couch, snoring loudly. I tiptoed out the back door, where the '76 Land Cruiser, which had been my parents' and which Jane and Dennis paid a fortune to keep running, was warming up. I climbed into the passenger seat and Jane handed me a thermos.

'Jesus, it's cold,' I said. 'Fucking Christ.'

'Please don't take the Lord's name, et cetera,' said Jane.

'Since when are you religious?' I asked.

'Since I don't know,' said Jane. 'It helps me personally, and it helps me figure out what to tell the kids when a pet dies.'

I nodded, smiling. 'Raven, Hammy the hamster, the betta fish . . . '

'All living happily in heaven,' said Jane.

'With Mom, I gather,' I said.

'With Mom,' said Jane. 'Who watches over us.'

'I wish I could believe that,' I said morosely.

'It's not so hard,' said Jane. 'Just believe it.'

'Then why did you lose the baby?' I said, anger rising in my gut. 'And why did I, if there's some benevolent God and a heaven?'

'I don't know,' said Jane.

We drove out of town in silence, taking County Road 14 past Lake Lenore into the national forest. We passed the remains of Ash, a town founded by the owners of the Bachelor Mine, and crossed Dexter Creek. Jane pulled the truck over. 'I'll do it,' I said.

'Thanks,' said Jane.

I climbed out of the truck. In the chilly morning, I knelt to turn the knobs on the front wheels that would lock the hubs and engage the four-wheel drive. I got back inside, and Jane put the truck in gear and drove up the steep dirt road to the Wedge

Mine. 'I always feel like we're going to fall off,' I said, grabbing the dashboard as Jane expertly handled a sharp switchback.

Jane sighed.

'What?' I said.

'That about sums it up,' said Jane.

'What does that mean?' I said.

Jane bit her lip and did not answer. In the dawn light, with her hair tucked under a Ouray High cap, she looked sixteen again, and I remembered how ethereal she had been, always pale, dreamy-eyed, sort of floating on the outskirts of our family. Before Dennis and the kids had worn her down, she'd been a blond angel.

'I used to think you looked like an angel,' I said.

'Not anymore?' she said slyly.

'No, but . . . ' I said.

'I don't mind being a fat mom,' she said matter-of-factly. 'Nobody saw me when I was perfect. I was invisible. Now I'm in the middle of everything. I'm the anchor.'

'The heart,' I said, moved.

'Yup,' said Jane. She put her shoulders back, and I saw in this gesture how proud she was of what she'd accomplished.

'I'm proud of you,' I said.

'Thanks. I'm proud of you, too,' said Jane.

'For what?'

'For accepting your life,' she said. I was silent, chewing that one over. I hadn't accepted my life at all, which was the problem, I saw now. But wasn't striving for your dreams supposed to be a good thing?

'I haven't accepted it,' I said.

Jane drove to the trailhead and pulled the brake. She gathered our backpacks, which she'd filled with sandwiches, trail mix, and lemonade. 'Let's go,' she said.

'Hold on,' I said. 'I *said* I haven't accepted it. I want a baby and I fucking deserve one, just as much as you do.'

'Okay,' said Jane. 'You're right.'

'Damn right I'm right,' I said, jumping out of the Toyota, my feet landing hard on the cold ground. I shouldered my pack and began walking along the trail, pausing only to enter our names and the ungodly hour in the trail register. It was barely light.

Wordlessly we hiked through aspen, spruce, and fir. I was fueled by rage and unhappiness, and I moved quickly. My thighs burned, and I soon left my sister behind. I reached the meadow and stopped, sitting on a boulder to wait for Jane. I took in the view — there was Ouray, looking like a doll-sized town from twenty-five hundred vertical feet above. As I looked out at the Red Mountains and Hayden Peak, I remembered hiking this same trail with my parents, Jane in a pack on my dad's shoulders. I must have been six or seven. When my mom said, 'Keep going to the Bridge of Heaven,' I'd been scared and stopped short.

'I don't wanna go to heaven,' I protested.

'It's not the real heaven,' my mom said.

'Bet the real heaven looks a lot like it,' Dad said, adjusting his pack.

'Oh, no,' Mom said. 'The real heaven looks like this.' She'd taken my hand and Jane's and kissed my dad.

'Such a softie,' Dad said, smiling.

'Come on, honeybun,' Mom said to me, tugging me forward.

★   ★   ★

Jane finally reached me, breathing heavily. 'I don't feel so good,' she said, reaching into her pack for a water bottle and peanuts. 'This might have been a better idea in theory.'

'You can do it,' I said. 'But it's okay if you don't want to.'

'I wanted to say goodbye to her there,' said Jane.

'What?' I said, thinking of my mother.

'It was a girl.'

Jane sat next to me on the boulder. This felt like a good time to say what I needed to say. 'Jane,' I began, 'if you get the test, you'll be able to take preventative measures. I just think it's something you need to do.'

'We're all going to die, Alice,' said Jane, pulling her knees up.

'Okay,' I said, 'but for the kids' sake, I just think — '

'Number one, it's none of your business,' said Jane. 'Okay? I'm not an idiot, and I'm not naive. I understand how it all works. I get the brochures you send in the mail. But . . . I want to live. Just move forward. I don't want to try to . . . shape everything to my will with a fucking hammer.'

'A fucking hammer?' I said.

'If I had known I'd lose this baby,' said Jane, tearing up, 'I wouldn't have felt her feet kicking inside me.' Her eyes grew damp. 'I got to feel my daughter's kicks, and they felt like butterflies.'

I frowned and opened my mouth, but Jane stood quickly and continued up the trail. We hiked for three more hours without saying a word, finally reaching the highest ridge. On the Bridge of Heaven, Jane reached her arms up to the sky. 'Goodbye, my baby girl,' she said. She began to sob — raw, wrenching cries.

'It's okay,' I said, holding her, starting to cry myself.

'It's not okay,' said Jane. 'But it's the way it is.'

Her words hit something inside me, something hard and cold. I felt as if I had been punched. I thought about holding Mitchell, when I'd thought he was mine. I'd touched his face with my nose, breathing him in. And then, hours later, I relinquished him, and was left by myself in his room, staring at the crib.

But standing on the Bridge of Heaven next to my sister, my memory shifted. I hadn't been alone, in truth. Jake had been there, next to the crib, just out of focus. His heart was as shattered as my own, and I had not even seen him.

'It's the way it is,' I repeated.

And Jane repeated, 'Goodbye.'

43

Carla

My first morning in America was just as I'd dreamed it would be. My mother did not go to work at the Texas Chicken restaurant. She stayed with me, cooking tortillas, beans, and stew on the hot plate in the corner of the room. She sang and let me sleep all day in one of the two beds. Whenever I woke, she fed me, the savory *sopa de mondongo* like happiness on a metal spoon. She stroked my face, repeating, '*Mi bebé, mi bebé,*' and when my brother Carlos came home from school, he pounced on me like an overgrown dog, hugging me and looking so big and easy in his sweatsuit made of nylon material.

It was then that my perfect day concluded, because at this point I was introduced to my new sister, one-year-old Marisol; her father, my mother's boyfriend, Mario; and the two other families who lived with us in Room Sixteen.

I would never sleep in a bed after that first morning. My mother took me on the bus to Fiesta Mart, where I chose a Dora the

Explorer sleeping bag and three stuffed animals, and we carried them back to the Ace Motel. I made a place next to my brother on the floor. It seemed fun — like a game — for the first few nights. The television was always on and the other families had a total of seven children, so it was very loud. At night I tried not to hear the arguments, financial discussions, and sexual relations inside our room, and the drunkards and drug addicts who congregated in the Ace Motel parking lot.

My mother asked me about Junior only once more. We were alone in Room Sixteen, a rare event. 'I know what happened to Junior was what God wanted,' my mother began. 'I am thankful for all that He has given me. I am thankful He brought you to me in Texas.' She looked down at her clasped hands and managed, her voice thick with unshed tears, 'I cannot help but ask you, Carla: *why?*'

I told her what had happened, confessed that I had climbed into the *combi* when I should have waited. My mother held me and rocked back and forth, a low cry coming from her throat, the sound of a heart breaking. My face pressed to her chest, I became hot with fury. 'You left me alone in Tegu,' I said, pulling away from Mami. 'I asked you to come home and you didn't come. I could not fight the Resistol! I did my best!'

My mother put her head in her hands. When she raised it, I saw how unkind America had been to her. Her face was lined. Underneath her eyes, the skin was grayish. She stared into a middle distance, as if lost herself. She was a woman who maybe should have stayed. 'There is no use in regret,' she said unconvincingly.

'What does that mean?' I said. 'Why did you never send for me?'

'This is God's plan,' said my mother.

'Do you really believe that?' I said. 'God's plan is for Junior to be lost in Mexico?'

'We cannot understand His ways,' said my mother. 'We can only have faith. God brought you to me. God will watch over Junior.' Her eyes glittered. Her jaw clenched with the effort of believing the only thing she could believe.

'He is probably dead,' I said.

Her face blazed and she raised her hand to slap me, but stopped herself. Her arm fell to her side. She closed her fingers around the cross she wore on a chain around her neck. 'If he is dead,' she said. 'If he is . . . if he is . . . ' She could not finish. Her faith, I saw then, was a rope dangling above an abyss of despair. She could hold on to the rope or let go. Finally she concluded weakly, 'We will all be together in heaven.'

I felt both admiration and pity as I stared at her. She tightened her embrace. 'We will be together,' she whispered. I relaxed into my mother. She believed it, she believed it, she believed it.

★ ★ ★

But America! It was easy (too easy?) to distract yourself from weighty matters here. Everything was so bright — it was as if stores had more light bulbs than the ones at home. The streets were very wide and there was no trash on the ground. There seemed to be endless space — supersized restaurants; huge cars; fat white, black, and brown people eating triple-decker hamburgers.

My mother told me that when she first came to Texas, the only food she knew how to order in English was a hamburger. 'I ate so many I could not eat another,' she said. But then McDonald's started numbering the meals — it was the best thing to happen in her life! 'I could order a Number Six!' she exclaimed, 'I could have anything — fish, chicken, the McRib sandwich!' My mother was chubby, and I looked forward to becoming as plump as an American myself.

My first week in America, we walked to McDonald's, and when we got there she told me to order whatever I wanted. I chose a meal with two meat patties and cheese and sauces and pickles. We waited for a Guatemalan man to wipe our table with a rag and then we sat down and I bit into my Big Mac. It was so delicious I could hardly believe it was real, but I still found room to eat every single french fry in my bright red french fry holder. Even Coca-Cola tasted fatter in America.

My mother brought me with her to work at the Texas Chicken. It was not as I had envisioned. My mother did not wear a banana-colored uniform. She wore elastic pants and a shirt that grew dirty as she stood over hot vats of oil transforming frozen things into hot, delicious things. Pieces of hair fell out of her net and she brushed them back with the top of her hand, but she could not stop working long enough to readjust the net or find a bobby pin. The sight of her cheeks growing red and the way her hair kept falling back in her eyes made me not only sad but actually sick, and I went into the bathroom and vomited. Then another Honduran woman came and cleaned the toilet with a rag and a bottle of sanitizer.

My mother was paid $7.25 per hour. She was allowed to pee twice during her eight-hour shift. My head spun when I thought about how long it must have taken her to earn the two thousand dollars I had given to the Snake. (Carlos told me later that she had sold her car to get the money, a car she had saved for years to buy.)

After my mother's day at Texas Chicken, we rode the bus back to Room Sixteen. My brother and his friends and the other families were sprawled around the room like laundry. 'Ma, you gotta pack me a better lunch than PB&J,' said Carlos, his voice loud and obnoxious. 'I already told you I don't like peanut butter!'

My mother nodded and smiled in an indulgent way, and I hated Carlos right then. I hated him even more when he made a mistake in his video game and said, 'Fuck!' and threw the controller at the TV, making my mother wince.

I could not stay inside Room Sixteen, and I could not go outside Room Sixteen because the Ace Motel had some bad elements, my mother said. Her boyfriend, Mario, worked behind the meat counter at the HEB grocery store, and we did have plenty of meat that was still perfectly delicious even though the date on the package said it had expired.

My new sister, Marisol, was dreamy and sweet, an American citizen and someone who had never known anything sad or difficult besides how loud it was in Room Sixteen. She only had a few words and none of them were Spanish. She grabbed one of my three stuffed animals (the elephant), and when I asked for it back, Mario said, 'Don't pick on your little sister, Carla! For Christ's sake, get over it, you're twelve!'

Before work one day, my mother took me to a giant American high school. Carefully, she filled out the paperwork that would enroll me in sixth grade. I was too old to go to the elementary school with Carlos. When I told Carlos I was scared to attend the middle school and did not speak any English, so I did not know how I would ever know what the teachers were talking about, Carlos said, 'You will learn, and I will tell my friends to keep you safe.'

I did not ask, *What friends?*, and I also did not ask, *Safe from what?*

★   ★   ★

One evening, we went to a green park. Mario brought charcoal and ingredients for a picnic. Carlos played *futbol* with older boys and then joined me under a live oak tree. 'Can I ask you about my brother?' he said to me under the tree.

'He is my brother, too,' I said. I put on the

281

sunglasses I had found on one of the tables at the Texas Chicken.

'I know,' said Carlos.

'He was sniffing the Resistol,' I said.

Carlos's eyes bored into me. 'How could you leave him behind?' he said. 'I just don't understand.'

I ripped a dandelion out of the ground. 'He made it to Ixtapec,' I said. 'I was caught and he ran away. I found him in a shelter there. A man offered a ride in a *combi*, and Junior was not there when the ride was leaving.'

'So you abandoned my brother,' said Carlos. He stared at me, waiting. When I did not respond, could not find words to respond, he stood up and ran to join the games with the other children who looked like me but who were nothing like me at all.

'He is my brother, too,' I told the live oak tree.

44

Alice

I booked a flight home the next day. Jane was doing fine with her big and small boys around her, and I missed Jake and the restaurant and my friends and the swampy smell of Austin and its buttery, sumptuous light. When I called Jake to give him my arrival info, he answered his phone with a whisper, 'Hey, can't talk, I'm at Dillard's.'

'What?' I said. 'What are you doing at Dillard's?'

'We already tried Forever 21, the Limited, and Macy's,' Jake said. 'Evian can't find the perfect dress. It's a freaking disaster.'

'You took Evian to the *mall*?'

'You weren't here and her mom had to work,' said Jake matter-of-factly. 'She can't go to Homecoming in a *sack*.'

'So Marion's going ahead with Homecoming?'

'I don't know.' Jake's voice dropped again. 'But I don't want to be the one to tell Evian, and that's for damn sure.'

I heard Evian's voice in the background,

bossy and loud: 'Jake! Are you even *looking* at this dress?'

'I am!' called Jake. 'Hold the phone, Evian, I think that's the one!' To me, he said quickly, 'Got to run, honey. I'll see you tonight.'

'Okay,' I said. 'Jake . . . ?'

But his attention was diverted back to Evian. 'I'm not sure about the sequined headpiece,' I heard him say, and then the phone cut off.

★ ★ ★

Jake and Pete were waiting for me in the truck outside Austin-Bergstrom Airport. 'I missed you so much,' I said, bending down to the passenger window to hug my dog.

'Hey,' protested Jake from the driver's seat.

'You the most,' I said, climbing into the truck, scooting Pete to the backseat, and kissing Jake. He kissed me back, then handed me some pieces of paper stapled together.

'Hot off the presses,' he said.

'Oh,' I said. 'The *Bon Appétit*?'

He waited, his eyes bright and trained on me. I looked down. In the grainy mock-up his agent had faxed, there was my husband in jeans and a dark shirt, standing with his boots crossed next to the pit. The caption read, 'Best Barbecue in America? *Bon Appétit*

284

Talks to Jake Conroe, Rising Star.'

'Rising star?' I said. 'My God, honey! Look at you! Look at your hair!'

'They did it for me,' said Jake. 'That's called 'product' in there.'

'I'm so proud of you,' I said. And I felt it, too, coursing through me — pride and gratitude. 'You're a rising star.'

'True,' said Jake.

A security guard rapped on the truck. 'Move along,' she said.

I opened the window, holding up the fax. 'Look!' I said. 'That's him! That's Jake Conroe!'

'I don't care if you're Lyle Lovett,' said the woman. 'Move along!'

'Take me to bed, hon,' I said.

'Whoa,' said the guard.

'You heard me,' I said. Jake hit the gas.

★　★　★

On the way home, I tried to apologize. 'I'm going to try not to be such a . . . '

'Meddler?' he suggested.

'Jeez!' I said. 'Such a . . . '

'Instigator? Tyrant? Stone-cold fox?'

'You know me pretty well,' I said.

'I do.'

'Jane's sad, but she's going to be okay.'

285

'How about you?' said Jake.

'It's hard,' I said. 'I still want a baby. I'm not going to lie to you, honey.'

Jake turned onto Mildred Street. 'I know,' he said. 'I still want one, too.'

'You do?' I said.

'Of course I do,' said Jake. 'But you know . . . ' His voice trailed off. 'I don't have a great statement here,' he said finally. 'I don't have a moving conclusion.'

'Me neither,' I said. 'It hurts, to want something you can't have.'

'Yeah,' said Jake. He parked in front of our house, and I looked at his face, his ruddy skin. He smelled of barbecue and soap. I had always thought we'd be a family by now, but here we were, and it wasn't nothing, what we had. It was a lot. I leaned into him, my sweet one.

45

Carla

I went to the American high school for three months. The teachers were kind to me, although I did not understand most of what they said. Before school, in between classes, and after school as I waited for the bus, I was nervous — not in the harrowing way I had been scared on The Beast, but in a more aching way. I was frightened of being singled out or ridiculed. I wanted so much to be noticed, and I also wanted to disappear.

Even in Room Sixteen, I was lonely. My mother stopped paying special attention to me. I began to feel angry at all the other children (including my new sister and Carlos), who had not been left behind in Tegu. I hated being sent to the Laundromat. I hated feeling sick all the time, and I hated the used clothes my mother brought me from Savers. I missed Humberto and wrote him endless letters in my school notebook. I would make something of myself, I decided, and then I would go back to Tegu with enough money to save us both. In the middle of the night, I prayed to God that Humberto would never know what had happened to me on the train. I prayed for God to make me a virgin again.

One night I heard my mother and Mario arguing in English, which meant they were talking about me. My mother was saying, 'No, no, it can't be true.'

Mario said, 'Look at her, *amor*! Are you blind?'

Their words escalated in intensity and everyone else in Room Sixteen pretended to be asleep. I pressed my eyes shut and prayed. In the morning, my mother took me on the bus to a medical clinic. When the test results came back, she said, 'Carla, who did this to you?'

I bowed my head in shame and told her what had happened at night on The Beast.

She looked very sad and shook her head. 'I will speak to my boss at the Texas Chicken,' she said. 'You can work until the baby comes, and then I just don't know.'

46

Alice

A hush fell over our restaurant as Marion walked in front of the crowd. Since the Chávez gymnasium had been closed down due to the discovery of asbestos beneath the floorboards, Marion had had to use any place she could find to convene school meetings. And this was an important one. Marion, wearing a yellow pantsuit with her gold jaguar pin, cleared her throat. 'Hello, everyone,' she said in English and then in Spanish. 'Good evening.'

We had no sound system, so Marion had to raise her voice to be heard. The crowd had a few white members, but most Chávez parents were Latino and black. 'Are you closing Johnson down?' yelled a heavyset man in the back.

Marion raised her hand. The group fell silent. 'As most of you know, I am fighting my hardest to keep Chávez Memorial open. If some of you have heard rumors about a van coming to get your student if they're marked absent, I can confirm that those rumors are *true*. I've got a *van* and a *GPS unit*, and I have your *addresses*. So get your kids to school.' This announcement was met with laughter and encouraging shouts.

She took a breath. 'We have a big fight ahead of us. We have the TAKS tests coming up this spring, and I believe that we will raise our scores enough to keep this school open. Chávez has the smartest kids in town, and I also want you to know I believe we have the *best-looking* kids in town.' At this, Sam, who was sitting by the kitchen with Evian, yelled, 'You know it!'

'That's enough from the peanut gallery,' said Marion, adjusting her glasses. 'I have called you all here tonight to talk about the Homecoming football game and dance.' The room became silent. Jake put his hand on my knee and squeezed.

'Now, this isn't an easy thing to say,' said Marion. 'I was a teenager myself, and I know how . . . ' Her voice broke, but she regained control and continued, 'I know how very much this night means to our kids.' She took a deep inhale. 'The Austin Police Department has offered me extra security at the football field. We are taking a risk — a big risk — but I trust your children,' she said. 'We have to trust them. We have to believe in them. And I'll be honest, I'm scared someone's going to do something stupid. I'm afraid. But I choose trust over fear. The Homecoming football game will go on as scheduled this Friday night.'

Cheers erupted, and the parents — some of whom had played for the Jaguars themselves — began to sing the Johnson Jaguars fight song. Marion bowed her head and let the applause roll over her. Jake whispered, 'Wait till you see Evian's dress!' I smiled and shook my head.

'I'm not finished,' continued Marion. The crowd settled down, and Marion spoke. 'I'm very sorry to say what I have to say next. But I haven't been able to find a solution, I haven't, and so I just . . . ' She put her shoulders back, lifted her head, and spoke. 'There will be no Homecoming dance after the game. The gymnasium is unfit, and we don't have anything left in the budget for the rental of an event space, much less money for food, music . . . ' Her voice trailed off. 'We will have the game,' she said, 'and I hate to send the kids out into the street afterward, but I don't know what else to do.' She nodded firmly, and though the crestfallen group was utterly quiet, she said no more.

I felt the sadness around us — it was a real thing, like toxic gas. People's shoulders fell forward, and sighs were audible. 'It's not

Homecoming without a dance,' whispered one mother.

'It'll have to be,' said another. 'It'll just have to be.'

People began to gather their things. I saw Evian's mom at her side, consoling her. Out of habit, I tried to think of how I could fix things, what I could do, but it seemed there was no damn solution — this disappointment just was the way it was.

Someone pushed open the front door, and I felt a breeze on my face. I turned to my husband, but he wasn't sitting next to me. Scanning the room, I saw him climbing on a chair. I frowned.

'Stop!' cried Jake 'Wait! Don't go!' The most famous man in Austin (this week) yelled at the top of his lungs, 'Listen to me!' People turned toward Jake and listened.

'I'm Jake Conroe,' he said. 'This is my restaurant, mine and my wife's. That's her, my wife, that's Alice.' I lifted my arm, confused.

'We care about your school,' said Jake. He wasn't a man who liked public speaking, so I worried a bit for him, standing up there. None of these people needed our sympathy. 'We care about Marion, and also we care about kids who deserve a party. And your kids deserve a party!'

People began to clap, and I joined them. We all waited for the nice white guy to step down. But Jake wasn't finished.

'We'd like to offer Conroe's for the dance,' said Jake. 'We'll cover the food, and I'll find a DJ. If you want it, you can have it.'

I wasn't the only one who broke into a stunned smile. People exchanged glances, excitement gathering. 'So the question, I guess,' said Jake. 'The question is, do you want it?'

'Hell, yeah, we want it!' yelled a tall, skinny man in a T-shirt that said 'Austin Fest.'

'We want it!' echoed another.

The room erupted in cheers. Jake made his way back to me and took my hand. 'I think these people want a party,' he said.

47

Carla

In my last weeks of pregnancy, I was fired from the Texas Chicken for being too slow and needing too many bathroom breaks. I started taking long walks around Austin, Texas, just to get away from Room Sixteen. When the baby came, I would spend all my time in there, I knew. I would be trapped in the Ace Motel until the baby was old enough to be left in one of the day cares near the Ace Motel, and then I would go back to work lifting metal baskets in and out of boiling oil, if not at the Texas Chicken then at another restaurant. I supposed I should be thankful. I supposed this was the American dream.

It was fall. Most days I wore large T-shirts from Savers with a pair of elastic-waist shorts and sneakers. I was sweaty all the time. I understood I could never go back to Humberto — that beautiful, imaginary life was a mirage. I tried to accept my fate.

The baby turned somersaults inside me. It didn't know it was destined to grow up in Room Sixteen. Maybe the baby would have a better future than me, as we were allegedly in the land of limitless possibility. But when I was out of sight of anyone who knew me, I cried, my grip on any sort of faith weak.

My family treated me like the burden I had become. Carlos was embarrassed to be seen with me, and Marisol steered clear and did not return my stuffed elephant. My mother said that the baby could sleep next to me in my Dora the Explorer sleeping bag. She took me to parenting classes, where I knelt next to other girls and women and learned how to swaddle a plastic baby, how to burp it and change its diapers.

I didn't want the baby. But when I told my mother once, she said, 'How dare you say that! This is God's plan for you, and you will make the best of it.'

So I walked. As invisible as if I were magic, I passed houses, restaurants, and schools. I spoke to no one, but I felt every person's pain. The man waiting for a bus was disappointed. The girls playing jump rope were hungry. The woman in a brand-new minivan stared at her Internet phone while her children hollered from the backseat, hoping she would notice them. The dog tied up outside a fancy coffee shop looked at me, and I felt its misery as if I were the one yoked to a utility pole.

One night I smelled something wonderful. I was near downtown, east of Interstate 35. This was a part of town that was interesting to me — some blocks looked expensive and were filled with white college students who had funny hairstyles and beautiful clothes, and then right down the road would be a cantina with *ficheras* as covered in makeup as the ones I had seen in Ixtapec. Italian scooters were parked next to trucks with Mexican license plates. Although I felt like there was nothing new to see sometimes, in this part of Austin I was sometimes surprised.

It was night-time. My back was not hurting as much as usual. I bought an *agua fresca* from a street vendor and approached the building that smelled so delicious. It was a barbecue restaurant. Inside, I could see people dancing.

I drew closer, holding my breath. I could hear music from a DJ table in the corner. At the doorway to the restaurant, older people stood in throngs, laughing and sipping from plastic cups.

I was still in the dark. No one could see me. At times like this, I felt that I barely existed, my visions simply a fever dream. Only the thumps of my baby's feet could bring me back to myself. On this occasion, my baby was motionless, and must have been asleep.

A girl stepped outside the barbecue restaurant. She was a few years older than me, her dress the bright pink of a hibiscus in bloom. She wore a plastic tiara and a sash that spelled out 'Chávez Memorial Homecoming Queen.' In her hand was one long-stemmed rose.

I wanted the girl's hair. I wanted the lipstick that matched her dress, I wanted the dress. I wanted her slim ankles and her silver shoes and her big metal earrings. She thought she was alone, and she held the rose to her face, inhaling, looking heavenward. She was thanking God, I knew.

I began to cry. My own hair was dirty and fastened with a rubber band. My shoes were hideous, my T-shirt enormous. I had come so far on the strength of my will, but there was no way I could be Homecoming queen unless I gave up my baby. There was no way my *baby* would be Homecoming queen if she grew up in the Ace Motel with a mother who did not want her.

I knew how it felt to understand you had ruined your mother's life.

I thought of my grandmother and grandfather, who had raised their baby in a small shack on the outskirts of Tegu. My grandmother had scarcely been apart from my mother for an hour before my mother left for America. This was how it should be: a mother and child, enough food, time for kindness. A mother's lilting song as you fell asleep on the pallet, her hands scooping you up if you fell walking to the market, an orange shared at the table during a lazy afternoon, each bite the taste of sunshine. A mother who looked at you as if you were her happiness. This was what I wished for my baby — this was what I wished for myself.

I wanted my baby to have a mother who was well-rested enough to love, who could feel joy in motherhood and not just a weary, relentless obligation. My heart was sick with the wanting. And I could not give my baby this life, no matter how many hours I wiped toilets or fried potatoes at the Texas Chicken.

The Homecoming queen was illuminated like a saint, shining in her hibiscus dress. I watched her from the shadows, gazing at this girl in her most private, most perfect moment. My vision blurred, and I fell to my knees. I saw it then — I understood God's plan for me. I turned my own face up, and, with the Homecoming queen, I gave thanks.

48

Alice

I was frozen in the Conroe's BBQ restroom. I could hear the thumping beat of an unfamiliar song, and the shrieks of teenage girls. I counted the rolls of toilet paper again: twenty-seven. I checked the liquid soap dispenser: full. From the cabinet underneath the sink I brought out the Windex and sprayed, then carefully polished the mirror.

The police had been circling the block all night. As the Chávez students danced and preened, made out and bumped hips and dirty-danced in full view of the hapless chaperones, the rest of us waited for some nut job to pull out a gun. Even Jake, in his Goodwill tuxedo with the ruffled shirt and neon cummerbund, even he looked jumpy, but maybe he was just worn out from assembling three hundred Sweet Stacy sandwiches.

The punch could be spiked, some kid could OD, Sam might dump Evian and ruin what was quite possibly the best night of her life. I stood in the john, trying to think of something else I could sanitize.

I reapplied my creamy lipstick. I gazed at the wrist bouquet that matched Jake's. I brushed my hair and sprayed it with the can of Aqua Net. I thought I should sweep, but the broom was all the way in the kitchen. Someone knocked on the door.

There I was, Alice Conroe. In a strapless dress, wiping. There was my hand, the skin loose around my knuckles. There was my mastectomy scar, barely visible when I reached to clean the upper corners of the frame.

I looked like an adult who knew things. *This is it*, I told myself, not sure what I was getting at. I understood I needed to return to the restaurant, where Beau was indulging his fantasies of being a DJ, if just for the night.

It occurred to me that so much of what I did — the cleaning, the futzing, the worrying about everyone I loved — was born of my childhood belief that if I kept in motion, I would not have to miss my mother. So much of what we *all* did, to be fair, was a valiant attempt to distract ourselves from the fact that we were going to die, and none of us knew when or how or what the fuck we should do with ourselves in the meantime.

I took a breath. I had to just show up and feel everything — to risk the possibility that despite Marion's heroic efforts Chávez

Memorial would shut down in the spring (it would), to endure the painful hope that Jake might let us keep our adoption file open a few months longer (he would), to swallow the reality that Jane might get cancer and there was nothing I could do about it (she would not). I had to stand by and watch as Evian ruined her own damn evening by spurning Sam and going home with a small-time drug dealer. I had to hold my husband, let myself burn for him, even though he could die or leave me or we could just lose our love as time went by.

I had to go out there into the Chávez Memorial High School Homecoming dance simply because I could: I was alive on this earth and my mother was not.

I had to leave the bathroom.

Another knock came. I put my hand on the knob and turned.

49

Carla

This essay has gone on for a long time, I am aware. We have a guidance counselor at our school, Mrs. Halpern. She means well, but when she tells us we must *follow the instructions to the letter*, I do not believe her. I want you to know me, Admissions Officer. I want you to understand what I have done so that I can attend the University of Texas, so that I can walk along the paths I see in your shiny catalog and join the group of students sitting in a circle of sunlight outside your library. If you admit me to your university and I find a way to make it from the desk where I am sitting to that circle of sunlight outside your library, the American dream will lie before me.

I can only imagine what sort of essays you will be reading. I have been told that American students will travel to my country to gain *life experience* and *empathy*. Maybe they will write about the little girls they see picking through trash at the dump in Tegucigalpa, handling discarded food to see if it is just a bit rotten, still edible. It is possible that an American in a tour bus saw me give putrid fruit to my brother, trying to save him from a hunger so unrelenting that he was forced to escape it with yellow glue. I don't know. I can't go back, in any case. I cannot board an airplane without documents.

In my years here in the Ace Motel, I have barely spoken to American kids. There is a new grocery across the street, which advertises 'real local food.' I went inside once, ogled things like couscous, almonds, and Texas peaches (picked by Ernesto, perhaps?). The cashier told me I was supposed to bring my own containers to fill and that this would help eliminate waste from the planet. I said, 'Like a bread bag?' and he laughed as if I had told a joke.

In the parking lot outside the room we share with two other families, we cook beans. Even the druggies (who never share a motel room with more than three others) look askance at us. They would be surprised to know I can use the word 'askance.'

I have worked hard to learn your language. Most of my relatives speak little English. I go to places where Americans congregate and speak loudly — shopping malls, Starbucks coffee bars, Subway sandwich shops. For the price of a drink, I listen to the way Americans speak, and there is even a clean, free bathroom. I can record the voices around me to play for myself later, the way as a child I played the songs of Stevie Wonder even after my batteries died.

I know how privilege sounds: haughty, a bit loud, incensed by imagined slights. Americans don't seem to laugh as much as we do, in my family. Maybe they haven't been forced to see the worst of human nature, to know the true value of joy.

On The Beast and in the shelters along its rails, people traded stories about their experiences. We talked about bandits, robbers, rape. We agreed that people were kindest in Veracruz and Oaxaca. Once, as I rode the train, a very old woman threw a blue plastic bag that landed in my lap. I opened the bag to find six rolls, a bottle of lemonade, and a sweater.

'Thank you!' I called, waving.

I heard her voice ring out in the distance: 'May God watch over you!' And so He has.

Now that we are here, we do not talk about The Beast.

★ ★ ★

I will finally answer the essay question you have posed: *What was the worst day of your*

304

life? You might be surprised to hear that the worst day of my life did not take place along the journey from Tegucigalpa to Austin, Texas. The worst day was not losing my brother Junior, though that was a very bad day. Being raped more than once was . . . I have no words. But it was not the worst.

★   ★   ★

I gave birth to a baby girl on November 3. The hospital was clean, and already decorated for Thanksgiving. Paper turkeys lined the hallways along with paper cutouts of cornucopias, which I learned the word for later and hope never to see again. My mother was very angry with me, but when my contractions began, she helped me to her boyfriend's truck and drove us south, to the address on the papers I had been given.

The labor pains were like a drill, boring to my very center. I was offered an epidural and I refused it, wanting to feel everything, knowing what was to come. But then the agony increased, and again I was offered an epidural, and I said yes. A doctor with a white mask covering his white face told me to push, push, and I pushed. But it was not enough. My mother spooned ice chips into my mouth. Her hand on my forehead. Her fingers in my hair. My mother: in spite of everything, she would take care of me.

My daughter was born in the hours between the middle of the night and the dawn. Her face is burned into my eyelids: whenever I sleep, or even blink, I see her. She had curls, night-black. Her eyes were a very pale brown, and her eyelashes were long and dark. She looked shocked to be in the world. She parted her lips and screamed.

They cleaned my daughter and wrapped her in a blanket with a pink cap on her head. Then they gave her to me. I kissed her, tried to take in her smell, to remember. A wave of longing caught me in its fist. *You can do it!* the wave told me. *It is not too late!* And I let myself have the fantasy of taking my daughter home to the Ace Motel, sleeping next to her (and my new sister and my brother) in my Dora the Explorer sleeping bag. Making her dinner in the parking lot, watching her run between the cars, dancing in the Texas sunshine. My mother pulled us both into her arms. 'It is a mistake,' she whispered. 'Do not give up your child.'

But I knew a different future was possible. I thought of opening a book in a circle of light next to a cream-colored building. I felt a backpack full of books on my shoulders, imagined a takeout cup of tea. Even in the hospital, moments after giving birth, I saw this version of myself and prayed that God would understand my decision.

And my daughter! She would not grow up in a room that smelled of sweat and beer and frustration and beans. She might even have her *own* room, all by herself, with a crib and a mobile from the Pottery Barn catalog I had once picked up at a Starbucks coffee bar. A crib that cost eight hundred and fifty U.S. dollars! And soft, thick blankets. And a mother — one of these American women — who did not have to make terrible choices. My girl would not have to struggle. She would not be hungry. No one would hold her down on the top of a train, shoving his seed into her, thrusting with anger and pain. I brought my lips to my baby's perfect rose of an ear. And like the old woman in Veracruz who had thrown me a bag of bread and lemonade, I said, 'May God watch over you.'

And then I gave her to the waiting nurses and signed the papers. I ate a hospital breakfast of scrambled eggs, toast, and a fruit cup. I slept for a while, and then I got out of the metal hospital bed, my breasts on fire, full of milk for no one. My mother helped me dress myself and settle into a wheelchair. We left the room.

As my mother pushed me toward the

elevator, an American couple entered through the doors at the end of the long hallway. They hurried toward the viewing room, and I knew. I saw them exchange a smile; the woman reached for the man's hand and they clasped fingers. The man wore a T-shirt that said 'University of Texas.'

As we passed them, the woman looked at me. Her face was clear and untroubled. She was shining with happiness.

And I was free.

I climbed into my mother's boyfriend's truck and she drove us home to the Ace Motel. No one spoke to us as we hurried into Room Sixteen. The men had gone to work, and my mother bathed me in the cracked tub. I can still remember the feel of the warm washcloth on the back of my neck. I tried to remind myself that I would recover, go to school, and make a bright life for myself in America. I would go to university and become a lawyer or a doctor. I would buy my mother a wonderful house. Maybe someday I could see my baby again. I had checked the box on the paper that said she could contact me. My body felt liquid. My daughter was gone. As my mother washed my hair, I cried with abandon, letting go.

This was the worst day of my life.

50

Alice

The paper turkeys on the wall flutter as we walk down the hospital hallway. Since my mother's death, I have always hated hospitals, but for some reason I am not scared this time. It's true: this birth mother could also change her mind, as Mitchell's did. We might be getting our hopes up only to have them dashed. But something has shifted in me. I don't know what will happen tomorrow, or ten minutes from now, but I am calm. A faded banner above the nurses' station (likely brought out every year) says, 'Be Thankful, for You Are Blessed.'

I reach for my husband's hand. It is warm.

A heavyset woman in a pink sweatshirt pushes a wheelchair past. The girl — no older than twelve — glances up. Her expression is so sad it stops my breath. I feel her sorrow enter me, slow and terrible. As she is wheeled toward the exit, the girl watches me over her shoulder. She reaches the end of the hallway, and when the door is opened, she turns from me, toward the light.

Jake has allowed me to pause. But now he squeezes my fingers — a question. I meet his eyes and nod.

There is a glass window a few feet ahead of us. I pull Jake forward. In the nursery, only one tiny cradle is occupied. Swaddled in a pink blanket, a baby is asleep. Her round face is so lovely. Jake pulls me close, his breathing ragged. 'There she is,' says Jake.

A woman approaches, her heels clicking smartly on the floor. 'Mr. and Mrs. Conroe?' she calls.

'Yes,' says Jake.

She reaches us and crosses her arms, staring, as we are, at the baby. 'Ah,' she says, 'I see you've found her.'

'Yes,' says Jake.

Machines whir and buzz, a strange lullaby. My blood roars in my ears. The baby girl yawns, showing us her petal of a tongue. And then she opens her eyes. They are caramel-colored. It seems she is looking at me.

Her cheeks, her curls, one tiny exposed fist! 'I've got you,' I whisper to my daughter.

She gazes at me for a moment, then exhales deeply and closes her eyes. Her tiny chest rises and falls as she finds her way to newborn dreams.

Acknowledgments

Without Alexia Rodriguez, who enabled me to meet immigrant children and to attend a Homecoming football game and dance, this book would not have been possible. Thank you so much, my dear friend.

The soul of this book comes from the work of Father Alejandro Solalinde Guerra, whose shelter, Hermanos en el Camino in Ciudad Ixtepec, Oaxaca, provides a safe place for migrants, offering them food, shelter, medical and psychological attention, and legal aid. His work and his words are the meaning of grace.

For the gift of time and glorious silence, I am tremendously grateful to Madroño Ranch, the MacDowell Colony, and the Corporation of Yaddo.

Michelle Tessler, your guidance, kindness, and encouragement mean everything to me. Also, thanks for the bourbon.

Kara Cesare, I am blessed to have your sharp editorial insight and your enthusiasm and love for my characters. You dream of Carlos and Junior, but every author dreams of an editor like you.

Many thanks to Ben Tisdel, Jenny Hart, Paula Disbrowe, Claiborne Smith, Stacy Franklin, Erin Kinard, Laurie Duncan, Dalia Azim, Mary Helen Specht, Erin Courtney, Samin Nosrat, Jodi Picoult, Dr. Joe Gonzales, John Mueller, Daniel Vaughn, Nina Schmidt Sells, Ellen Sussman, Leah Stewart, Jennifer Hershey, Kim Hovey, Libby McGuire, Gina Centrello, Benjamin Dreyer, Liza Bennigson, Sarah McKay, Mary-Anne and Peter Westley, Barbara and Larry Meckel, and my beloved barbecue research team, Nora, Harrison, Ash, and Tip Meckel.

Para todos los niños que han compartido sus historias conmigo: gracias por enseñarme el verdadero significado de la fe. Deseo que todos los que lean esta novela aprendan de su valentía, y que, un día, todos Uds. encuentren su hogar.

We do hope that you have enjoyed reading this large print book.

Did you know that all of our titles are available for purchase?

We publish a wide range of high quality large print books including:
Romances, Mysteries, Classics
General Fiction
Non Fiction and Westerns

Special interest titles available in large print are:
The Little Oxford Dictionary
Music Book
Song Book
Hymn Book
Service Book

Also available from us courtesy of Oxford University Press:
Young Readers' Dictionary
(large print edition)
Young Readers' Thesaurus
(large print edition)

For further information or a free brochure, please contact us at:
Ulverscroft Large Print Books Ltd.,
The Green, Bradgate Road, Anstey,
Leicester, LE7 7FU, England.
Tel: (00 44) 0116 236 4325
Fax: (00 44) 0116 234 0205

CLOSE YOUR EYES

Amanda Eyre Ward

What would you risk to bring the truth to light? On the night their mother was killed, Alex and Lauren were asleep in their backyard tree house. Their beloved father was sentenced to life imprisonment for the murder. Twenty-four years later, Lauren is a real estate agent who can't believe in love, and Alex is still trying to understand what happened to shatter his idyllic childhood. Only one stranger, a pregnant woman on the run from her boyfriend in Colorado, holds the clues that can free Lauren and Alex.